A Beauty Queen's Milli~~

G

By

Chapter 1

Treasure Matthews

This was what all my hard work, headaches, and bitching from my mother came down to. The moment I could possibly be crowned Miss Georgia.

This was something that was a long time coming and if anyone here deserved the title it would be me, Treasure Matthews, Miss Decatur County. Of course, every girl here would say that they worked hard and fought to get here, but I had truly been down a road half these girls couldn't survive. I was probably the only girl here that didn't have both parents in attendance and not because one died on something tragic. I was actually quite embarrassed as to why I only had my mother here to support me and never liked talking about where my father was.

That's because truthfully, he was my mother's rapist and was in Georgia State Penitentiary serving time.

Imagine how hard it was as a child to

answer the question as to where my father was.

When I would tell them Georgia State Prison,

everyone treated me as if I were the one locked

up for raping five women.

I wanted to hide my father's

truths so badly, but my mom made me wear it

on my forehead as a competitive boost.

Daughter of serial rapist competing for

state title.

She figured that would get me the sympathy vote if not anything. She said people would latch on to my underdog story. My mom struggled financially when I was a child and things only got better because my grandfather got sick, and she became his caretaker.

I liked to think if it wasn't for these competitions and dresses, we would've been able to afford a better life on our own and my mom could be happy. I watched her struggle to keep up with an image in public that tore her apart in private.

My mom was the true definition of a ghetto snob who tried to forget where she came from. The rest of her family still lived in the place she'd forbidden me to go even as an adult. How does that work? My mother was always more of a pageant coach to me than a parent. Her only goal in life was to see me become Miss America and marry rich.

"Here let me re-pin your sash, it's crooked and no Miss Georgia wears a crooked sash," she said sticking yet another sharp needle toward my body. I would never look perfect to my mama so I wished they would just call us to the stage. She would be adjusting things on me until Christmas if they let her.

"Mom, it's fine, I'm fine. Let me get in line," I said reassuring my mother who had nervous written across her face. I brushed down my pink sequined gown and gave myself one last look in the mirror.

You got this treasure.

We all lined up and walked to the stage. The crowd was cheering and the fake smile I had across my face was more irritating than the sequins itching my skin. I quickly scanned the crowd as we all stood there under the bright lights and saw everyone, that should've been here, except my boyfriend Chris. Where was he?

Chris and I had been together so long we used each other's deodorant and could brush our teeth in the restroom while the other one pooped. I felt we would get married one day; I just didn't know when that day would come. There were several times, he could've proposed but he didn't. Sometimes I felt Chris just wanted a beauty queen on his shoulder and would do the bare minimum to keep me.

He was my college sweetheart and doing a residency at the hospital now as Doctor Chris Samuels. I wasn't dumb when I picked him out of all the Omegas on campus. He was a dog true enough, but one I wanted to pet. I would wait on my ring as long as I had to because he was indeed a catch and quite fine, I may add.

"Treasure, I'm so nervous. I think it's between you and me," Kilani Jeffers, Miss Dekalb County said through her teeth as we smiled and waved at the audience.

I at that point snapped back to reality and realized I had no time to be looking for Chris. I'm sure he was here somewhere; he wouldn't miss the biggest day of my life for anything.

The host began to speak to the audience and dramatic music started to play. They would announce the runner-ups first and then the New Miss Georgia right after. I said a quick prayer and asked God to forgive me for any bad things I'd done in the past. All the lies I told to my mom growing up and all the things I'd snuck to do that she didn't

approve of. I know God made me this perfect, so he had to love me, right? I mean, he didn't give me a size two frame with a little booty for no reason.

The host kept us waiting and my stomach was in knots. I hadn't eaten in days and God knows I wouldn't eat for a couple more if I didn't win the title tonight. It took me days to form an appetite after I lost the Decatur County Pageant. I still remember the day I got the call saying the first winner was dead and the crown was mine. As ironic as it sounds, that's when I knew there really was a God.

How I got my county title is why half of the girls competing didn't take me seriously. They knew I was runner-up turned Miss Decatur, so I had so many people to prove wrong. I worked just as hard as everybody else and carried myself with pose and class. I knew I would someday be on this stage.

"The state finalists are," he said holding up the card and pausing dramatically as the music made our hearts race.

"Miss Dekalb County," he said as Kilani proudly stepped forward walking toward the front like the snob she was. I knew I didn't like that bitch the first day I met her, but I played along for my own image. Pageant girls were supposed to be sweet and dainty, not bougie and unlikeable like her. I immediately started to form envy in my heart seeing her walk to the front first as if she had everything in the bag.

"The next finalist is, Miss Atlanta," he said making me envy yet another contestant. This one I didn't have anything negative to say about which made me even madder. I took a deep breath and continued to smile because there was still one spot left.

"Last but not least. Our final finalist is, Miss Decatur." The host read and my knees buckled.

I wasn't tripping, right? I'd just heard my name being called as a finalist. God, please don't let this end like last time. I don't wanna be a runner-up and only at the Miss America Pageant because the first Miss Georgia gets murdered.

I walked up to the front as everyone from my family started to scream my name. It looked very ghetto, but what could I expect from a bunch of black people out of East Atlanta? My mom didn't want them here because she said they would embarrass her by acting a fool. They were my family though, ghetto or not; I loved my ghetto cousins and aunts.

As I stood in front, I tried to remember my posture and to smile while waiting on the judge's scorecard. My stomach was in knots, and I didn't know if it was from nerves or the abortion, I'd gotten just three months ago. Yes, it was true I wasn't perfect at all behind closed doors. I'd done the unthinkable to hide a secret and not be just another stereotype. Even though Chris was done with school I still had a life to live. I couldn't just drop out of the pageant because my belly was swollen. My mom would kill me and her grandchild and that I was positive about.

"Let's applaud our three finalists ladies and gentlemen. Let's give them a hand," the host said into the mic yet again snapping me out of a daze.

"Okay, the 2nd runner-up in the Miss Georgia pageant is, Miss Dekalb County," he said making Kilani's mouth drop to the floor after coming in third. Before I could even enjoy her shit face, Reagan grabbed my hands and mouthed 'Good luck beautiful,' being all sweet and shit. At that moment I looked into her eyes and stared deep into her soul trying to imagine what her life was like and how it was probably a cakewalk to get here. She was most likely seconds away from becoming Miss Georgia because her parents were rich and that wasn't fair.

She probably had a good mom and a father who loved her. A great boyfriend who paid attention and showed up to events instead of blowing it off. Before I knew it, I was hating on her so hard that I was squeezing her hands with a death grip. You could see that she was in pain, but she smiled through it like the pageant queen she was taught to be.

"Now for the moment of truth." The announcer said over the mic.

I was forcing a smile so hard right now; I wonder if people could tell. To think, I'd made it through the talent section, walking in floor-length gowns, and making sure I said all the right things while answering questions. Now I was almost to the finish line, and I couldn't stop. I had to keep going.

Please God, please God

"We have two beautiful ladies here tonight and only one crown," he said as we both looked at him with wide smiles.

"And the runner-up to the new Miss Georgia is..." he spoke as dramatic music played in the background.

"Miss Atlanta, which means Miss Decatur is your new Miss Georgia." I felt so lifted I couldn't believe my feet were still on the floor. The confetti began falling from the sky and I started crying like a baby.

"Treasure Matthews, come take your first walk as the new 2024 Miss Georgia." I was told and I walked forward barely able to stand from my emotions.

I knew God really did favor me. This was the happiest moment of my life. Nothing in this world could bring me down.

The chills still hadn't left my body and I'd been Miss Georgia for a few hours now. I'd taken so many pictures and given out so many hugs I was now ready to go home.

Coco my cousin, came walking up to me celebrating with her daughter on her hip. She was just as pretty as me and I was so happy to see her.

"Congratulations bih! You looked like a princess up there tonight. My baby was so happy to see her big cousin on that stage."

"Thank you! She's so pretty just like you. And girl that booty is the size of Georgia. That's the first thing I saw when I spotted y'all coming in tonight," I said as I pinched her huge butt. Big asses were something very common in the Matthews family. Even my skinny ass had something poking out in the back, which is why many early critics didn't think I was pageant girl material.

"Baby you were killing that dress and that performance. You sounded like us when we used to sing in the mirror." Coco and I laughed as we slapped hands.

"Yes, but that's before y'all got all hot and worried about boys." My mom chimed in making Coco roll her eyes.

"Aunt Lisa wasn't nobody worrying about boys."

"Mmhmm, if you say so Covovani. Treasure, don't you think you should be taking it in now? Remember I told you Chris got called back to the medical center for his residency so you will be walking in your house alone tonight. Unless you want me to stay with you?" she asked suggesting the worst possible thing that could happen after my good night. I need peace.

"No Mom it's okay. I told you the apartments are safe, it's a gated community. Plus, I'm safe all over Atlanta now. No one is going to hurt Miss Georgia."

"Yeah, well someone hurt Miss Decatur remember." She sang in a low tone, to make light of her fussing at me. Her passive-aggressive attitude gave her the ability to be the villain without looking like one. She often made suggestions for my life that we should've called final decisions because of how much weight they held.

"Well anyway cousin, congratulations again and I hope you can make it to her party. It would mean so much to Dream. Isn't that right baby?"

"Yes, you're so pretty." She smiled all innocently.

"Just let me know the exact time and I'm there," I replied hugging my closest cousin as my mom mugged like there was shit in the air. She couldn't stand how close I was to my cousin and tried her hardest to keep me away from Coco. All that trying still didn't work because we were now 22 and I still loved her. I didn't see Coco very often, but when I did it was a good time. I hadn't yet met a friend that was as genuine as her and to be honest I needed someone like her to always keep me grounded.

She never went to college but was a bomb ass hair braider who kept clients in and out of her house. That was success if you asked me because she got to make money without ever leaving her home.

"You sure you're going to be okay driving home? I can get a hotel room close to the venue tonight, darling."

"Mama, no I'm fine. Thank you, but I want to sleep in my bed. Plus, I want to see Chris as soon as he gets home. Whenever that is."

"I know I know," she said interrupting me as she grabbed both of my hands and held them tightly.

"Treasure, I'm so so proud of you. I mean, look at you, the new Miss Georgia. I've never been so proud. You finally made your mama happy," she said touching the beautiful diamond-studded tiara sitting on my head.

Those words, as messed up as the term finally made them, had me in another place. With the weight of the crown on my head, I was ecstatic without having to fake it and it felt good to finally have the approval of my mother. The only thing that would've made this night better was if Chris was here, but hopefully, he will be home soon.

I said goodbye to my family and got into my Malibu and drove off, finally feeling as if I could relax for the night. I turned up my music and headed to my small apartment in Buckhead to lie down as the 2024 Miss Georgia

When I drove into the parking lot, I checked for Chris's Charger in its usual place. Ever since he moved from campus, he'd been parking in my parking spot and forcing me to park five buildings over no matter the time of night. I grabbed my crown and sash and decided to leave my other items in the car until the morning. I had a straight shot to my first-floor apartment and took off through the parked cars.

I wasn't alarmed by anything unusual until I saw a car turn on its lights as I walked up. My heart started to race, and I started to walk faster feeling like I was now being watched. When I made it to my door, I was shaking so badly I couldn't get my keys out.

Once I finally did, I rushed inside the door like Diamond did when Myron was stalking her on Players Club. I had no idea why I was so scared, but I guess my mama had set that fear in my head by bringing up what happened after the last competition I lost. I needed to get that shit out of my head though, because no one was after me. I liked to hope I didn't have enemies like Jalani Smith.

I sat my bag down and then carefully placed my crown on the counter to stand back and look at it.

"Now if only I had the stand I ordered from Etsy. Actually, it was supposed to be here today," I said remembering I'd ordered a plastic stand to hold the crown I'd hoped to have. Yes, I was jumping the gun by ordering it before I was supposed to, but I didn't want to be in the situation I'm in now where I have a crown and nowhere to properly place it.

I smacked my lips and then went into my restroom to run some hot bath water and grabbed some lavender oil from the counter to add to my water. This is why Chris should've been here instead of at that stupid hospital. He could've been treating me like a princess on my big night and doing all of this stuff for me instead.

While waiting for my water to fill up the tub, I undressed and grabbed a towel from the hall closet, along with my silk robe from Victoria's Secret. I then got inside the warm water letting it continue to fill up around me.

"Now, let me see where my package is. I know I paid for one-day delivery," I said to myself as I logged onto Etsy. I put in my password and instantly got pissed seeing the package was marked as delivered and wasn't at my door. Well, maybe I just ran past it while I was thinking someone was after me. Now I was sitting in the tub debating on if I would go outside and get my package or get it after my long bath.

Let me just see if it's out there.

I thought to myself when I remembered I could easily check my Ring cam to see if UPS had been outside my door.

"Why is it rewinding so slowly? Let me just start the entire day over," I hit that automated option as I sat in the tub. I got a call from my mother who had timed me getting home almost perfectly, but I was not losing my spot on this surveillance. I got to 3:00 pm when I realized I hadn't seen Chris leave out yet. He told my mother he got called into the hospital at 9:00 this morning shortly after I left the house.

Not too long after the door camera read 4:30 pm, Chris came strolling out of the house, but he wasn't in hospital scrubs. This man was dressed up and wearing what he said he was going to wear to my competition today. He must've been on his way there when he got called in but why not say that though? Why lie about when you left the house?

I turned the water off before it overflowed and sprinkled a little more oil inside the tub to relax. Now I was about to call Chris because if he wasn't at work, I sure as hell should've heard from him by now.

Just as I started to exit the app, I saw a female walk up to the door with a car seat in her hand around 5:30 pm. She knocked on the door twice and then sat the car seat on the ground before running off. What the hell was happening at my apartment today? I was expecting a package, not a baby at my doorstep.

For some reason, my heart was racing watching that poor baby sit on the porch by herself. What kind of low-life Atlanta trash would do some shit like that? See it was mothers like her that made me appreciate my mom. She was batshit crazy, but at least she never left me on anybody's doorstep.

The baby sat outside for an hour before the camera showed Chris walking back to the door scratching his head.

"Fuck, why would she do this shit," he said before I watched him carry the baby into the house. Did he know this child? Where did that baby come from and who was the mama?

"Baby! Where are you at? Baby you here?"

I heard coming from the living room and I quickly got out of the tub. Chris was standing in the living room looking like the biggest fool with Walmart bags in one hand and to my surprise the baby in the other.

"What are you doing here with a baby?"

"Her mom left her here."

"Okay, but why did she leave her at our doorstep?"

"Man, I don't know. I'm trying to figure that out too."

"Chris stop playing with me. If you didn't know whose baby that was you wouldn't still have her. So, what's up? Is she yours?" I questioned as he stood there looking more and more like a lost puppy the longer I stared. He didn't even have to answer the question because I knew the answer with the baby still here. This was one of my worst nightmares happening on one of the best nights of my life.

"Un-fucking-believable! You went out, cheated, and got a baby Chris!" I said pointing at the baby as my voice started to crack from my emotions.

"This baby came from a mistake a while ago. I just found out she was mine today I swear!" Chris pleaded through his lying lips.

"Chris, how could you not only cheat but get a girl pregnant? You know how much shit I have to lose! A scandal like this could destroy me in the pageant world! Everyone on Instagram knows you're my boyfriend!"

"Here we go with that everyone on Instagram stuff. All you care about is how you look to people on the internet and the pageant world. Fuck that, I got real issues Treasure! Fitting into a dress is not my only issue like it is yours," he said downplaying what I worked hard as hell for. Chris loved the fact that I was a beauty queen but never missed a chance at downplaying it. He felt him being in a fraternity and medical school made his life that much more important than mine. He was at the top of his class at Morehouse and never passed up the opportunity to make himself seem smart. He was dumb as hell though; this situation right here just proves it.

"Yeah, you're right, you have issues, Chris. Ones that I'm not even dealing with anymore. You can have this shit. I'm done."

"That's fine Treasure, turn your back on me now that I'm low and you on a high since you Miss Georgia and everything," he said finally sitting the car seat and the bags to the floor like he was about to stay.

"What are you doing? You're not staying here tonight. You need to get your child and go." I said as Chris walked past me with bags going into the kitchen.

"Do you hear me? Get out! I can't even look at you right now," I said pointing toward the door as Chris continued to ignore me. It was like this nigga had turned off the volume on my mouth and tuned me completely out.

"Hello... do you hear me?" I asked crossing my arms while tilting my head to the side.

"Yeah, I can hear you, but I don't give a damn about what you are talking about. This is a situation we can not change," he said unloading diapers and formula from a bag.

"Wow! So, you just don't give a damn about how I feel?" I said getting emotional as I stood there.

"Look Treasure, your ass is going to have to deal with this because I have to deal with a lot for you."

"A lot for me? How! What?"

"Treasure, I keep a lot of shit to myself that would ruin that fake-ass image you and your mom try to portray."

"What fake ass image Chris? You're really going to sit here and insult me when you have another kid in my house right now!" I said becoming irate the more that Chris seemed to ignore my need for him to leave.

"What are you not understanding Christopher? You need to get out of my house now."

"Your house Treasure? I've been paying bills here, not you! I'm not going anywhere."

"Who cares if I am not paying the bills? This apartment is in my name and no baby is moving in here. Just go get somewhere else to live!" I yelled as Chris stood at the counter with his back to me. He was quiet for a moment before he decided to go so low he couldn't come back up.

"If you don't want your mom in prison by in the morning, you will leave me alone Treasure."

"Chris, what the hell are you talking about?"

"What am I talking about? Treasure, you know what I'm saying. I'll take that piece of shit crown away from you with one phone call."

"And how are you going to do that Chris?" I asked as he turned toward me.

"I'll call the police and tell them about your mother and Jalani Smith's murder. If you even think about leaving me, you won't be Miss nothing anymore and your mother will never see the light of day," he said sending an imaginary flame above my head. He pushed my crown off the counter as his threats to blackmail me continued.

"Don't throw my crown, are you crazy? And I don't care what you say, you wouldn't do that."

"Try me Treasure, I don't have shit else to lose."

"Umm, what about your residency and your freedom? I will tell them you helped my mom find the hit man. I will let them know y'all plotted to kill that girl behind my back and I found out after she was already dead! I had nothing to do with that so don't even try to take me down with you!" I said furious at how low Chris would stoop to make me stay with him.

The secret that lies inside me about Jalani was embedded so deep and I never liked to think about it. The fact that it was my mother and my boyfriend who found someone to kill that girl made me sick to my stomach. They did that behind my back and made me be okay with it even though it messed with me every night. Deep down inside, that's why my mother was always scared something would happen to me. I hate that Chris even got drunk and told me what they did one night. I still didn't even dare to bring it up to my mother.

"Chris, are you seriously going to turn all of this around on me and threaten me with something we all agreed would be a secret? You worked so hard in medical school and now you're a doctor. Would you seriously risk your job over me wanting to end our relationship?"

"Yeah, because there probably isn't going to be a job anymore anyway," he shrugged his shoulder.

"Why not?"

"Because a patient died yesterday when I didn't pay attention to what medicines he was allergic to. He was just 37 years old, and I killed him thinking about this baby's mama's threats she'd been sending me all week," he pointed at the baby.

"The hospital put me on administrative leave without pay. I have to meet with the board in two weeks, but I'm sure I'll never work as a doctor again," he said starting to cry dramatically like he needed to get it out. If he had told me about his job struggles yesterday, I would've been there for him, but tonight I just didn't care.

"The man that died had five kids; he just came into the hospital because he broke his arm. Treasure I really fucked up and you can't leave me right now," he said leaning against the counter with tears running down his face.

The baby was also crying as they did when they missed their mothers. I felt the baby's pain at that moment because I wanted to cry too. My fairytale night was over just like that, and it was back to the real world, only a worse world than I'd been in before.

Beauty queens had issues too, ours were just hidden behind make-up and fake smiles.

The next day

I had to be up before sunrise to go to my Miss Georgia photoshoot after barely getting any sleep last night. The doorstep baby was crying her lungs out and Chris nor I knew what to do with her or why she was so upset. After the nigga threatened to blackmail me, I went inside the room and locked the door crying my eyes out instead of basking in the joy of winning last night.

When I left the house, Chris was sitting on the sofa with the baby on his chest and his shoes still on. He looked defeated as hell, and I didn't feel sorry for his ass; I hope she cried until the sun set today. I knew I would be at this photoshoot all day and I was most likely staying at my mother's house tonight. She would be a lot easier to deal with than Chris and his screaming illegitimate child, that's for sure. I still couldn't believe the baby's mother abandoned her like that. Who the hell had Chris slept with?

I packed a bag and slipped out the door before he could even say goodbye. From there I headed down the freeway toward downtown to smile through my pain. The Atlanta traffic was already piled up and my morning coffee hadn't kicked in yet. I was about to look tired as hell on the website unless these bags under my eyes magically disappeared.

I drove up the freeway blasting Meg Thee Stallion trying to take my mind off of the bullshit. I wasn't letting Chris and his baby live rent-free in my head; I had better things to think about. I was wearing a beautiful crown on my head and would be competing on national television for the title I'd dreamed about my whole life.

My Instagram had been popping ever since I won, and The Shade Room posted a picture of me with a peach in the background for being the first black Miss Georgia. I'd gained 10,000 followers just overnight and already had a few fan pages pop up.

"Call from Coco," my phone said through the speakers interrupting my jam. I was about to ignore the call, but maybe she could help me get my mind off Chris for the moment.

One thing is for sure, Coco showed loyalty to me any time it was needed. I remember she beat up this girl at the park once for picking on me and threatened this chick over Facebook who liked the same guy as I did in high school. She was always the aggressive one and never played about me.

My mother however thought so low of Coco because she got pregnant young and fed into my mom's theory that Coco was too fast for me. Coco had Dream young and dropped out of high school to run the streets with her baby daddy, Deion, who looked good but was no good for anybody. Deion was your usual Atlanta knucklehead, turned rapper, who sold dope out of the studios he rented. To stay afloat, Coco had stripped, stolen clothes, and even sold drugs, all the while he had no real responsibilities. No, I wasn't too good for Coco, but I was damn sure too good for a nigga like Deion and taking care of a bullshit man.

One thing I used to be able to say about Chris was that he had his life together and always took care of me even through school. Now with that patient dying, that nigga was out of work just like Deion and planned on living with me with a child that wasn't mine. I guess she and I did have the same taste in men; I'd been dealing with an ain't shit man the whole time and I just didn't know it.

"Hey Miss Georgia!" Coco said after I finally hit accept on her call.

"Hey girl, what's up with you?"

"Nothing much chick, how about you? How does it feel to be the ultimate peach after last night's stunning victory?" Coco asked mimicking a reporter being her usual goofy self.

"Well, I can say it's been such an honor these past twelve hours being your new Miss Georgia. I promise to continue to represent my state with dignity and integrity as I take on this journey as your state's title holder," I replied as we began cracking up from my sarcastic scripted response.

"Girl I'm so happy for you! I was posting pictures of you all night. I'm surprised you even answered your phone because you never do. I said to myself, my cousin is a local celebrity now, so she probably really won't have time for me anymore" Coco called out my negligence.

"Yeah, I know cousin, but I promise I'll do better after this next go-round. My next pageant is my last, so I'll have plenty of extra time to do hood rat shit with you on a beach somewhere."

"Yes! Hopefully, you go out with a bang and take that crown home honey because I can't wait to tell bitches my cousin is Miss America."

"Girl, I hope so because no one will be able to tell me shit. So, what's going on? Where's my Dreamy?" I asked wanting to take the attention off me and ask about her for once.

"Oh, she's right here on her daddy's lap. We're all just sitting here waiting for my mama's food to be done. Dream, Treasure is on the phone."

"Tell her I said what's up." I heard Deion say in the background as he always did anytime me and Coco talked. He wasn't my favorite person because of what he did to my girl, but I guess he was okay when you looked at the bigger picture. He hadn't ever shown up to her house with an outside kid or threatened to expose her all while saying he lost his job. So, when you look at it, she had a pretty decent dude compared to mine.

"Tell him hi," I spoke back.

"We were actually calling because we really want you to attend Dream's birthday party that's coming up. She's been saying since last night she wants a Treasure-themed birthday party with you there. She really thinks you're a Disney princess girl,"

"Aww, that's so sweet. When is it? My schedule is about to be crazy preparing for Miss America and I-"

"It's whenever you have free time. You tell us," she said cutting me off, giving me no room to make an excuse.

"I mean, I may be free next weekend, but I will have to check my calendar to make sure. Where are you thinking about having it; Chuck E. Cheese, Catch Air, or something?"

"No girl, at my house in the backyard," she replied, confirming my worst fear. Coco lived in the hood, in one of Atlanta's worst neighborhoods, where crime and partying were an everyday thing.

"Those places I named are so fun. I went to Catch Air with Chris to one of his cousin's parties. We had a blast." I tried to convince her.

"Girl, my baby said she wants a swimming Treasure them party. I'm going to get like five small pools and fill them up with water for their asses and call it a day. That should be fun enough."

"Well, just let me know the official plans and I'll come," I said knowing that I would try to find every excuse not to show up next weekend. It truly wasn't because of them but because of my mama's mouth.

"Okay, thank you so much! I will owe you for life if you do this for real Treasure," she said, telling the baby I said yes, then handing her the phone.

"Say thank you." I could hear Coco whispering to Dream in the background and Deion asking,

"Is she coming for real?" With excitement in his voice.

"Thank you, Princess Treasure. I can't wait until my birthday party. I love you," she said in the most precious little voice ever. I sighed quietly thinking about the fucked-up position I was in having to disappoint this baby because I didn't want to be seen around her house.

I didn't want to mess anything up with Miss Georgia, but I also wanted to put good karma in the air. Maybe I could stop by for about an hour and go. What could it hurt spending a little time in the hood for a day? My mama didn't even have to know I was there.

Chapter 2

Coco

The next weekend

"Dream, stop running through this house and fix your skirt! You can't be cute for five minutes, I swear!" I yelled toward Dream's badass as I stirred in the cheese dip which was still hella thick for some reason. It was already going on 1:00 and I still hadn't even picked up Dream's cake from the bakery yet. You would think some of these grown motherfuckers hanging around would help, but everyone here was useless and already drinking at a kid's party. My baby daddy was the ringleader passing out shots like this was Freaknik.

"Damn baby, ain't none of that shit ready yet? Nigga hungrier than a muthafucka," Deion asked popping his head in the back door with a blunt still smoking in his hand.

"No! Nothing is done yet. Ain't nobody helping me with shit, so I'm behind on everything. I still gotta get her cake and blow up the rest of these fuckin balloons. Shit won't be done for a long time now!" I snapped never turning to face his inconsiderate ass.

"Damn, chill out, I can go get the cake. Why didn't you just say that? Mean fine ass."

"I shouldn't have to say anything Deion. She's your kid too and you haven't done shit all morning but scratch your ass, get a haircut, and get drunk."

"Damn a nigga had to look good at his baby's party and you know me, I'm going drink and scratch my ass every day," he said being his usual goofy self at the wrong time. He did actually look good with his crispy lineup and biceps poking out his muscle shirt. His light-skinned ass was covered in tattoos and fine as hell when he fixed himself up.

"But you're right baby. I will go get the cake, don't worry about that. I got you shawty."

"Okay so when are you leaving, because the party starts in an hour?"

"As soon you give me some of that cake," he replied smiling at me and licking his lips.

"No Deion, I don't have any time to fuck you. I'm running behind enough as it is."

"Come on baby, please. That ass looks like two stop signs in a sleeping bag. I gotta have you right now, come on; you know I won't last long." He kept tugging on my arm.

"Deion leave me alone. I told you not to get drunk before the party started. Now you're horny and wanna fuck," I said dismissing him and his crazy drunk ass sex drive.

"How can I leave you alone baby? That ass looks like my next meal in that dress. Actually, you need to take that shit off. If I'm looking, I know them niggas out there looking at all that peach cobbler too," he said grabbing my ass.

"Come on baby, you say the cheese dip is not done so I need something to hold me over until I can eat something else.

Here hit this. You stressing over a kid's party. Just relax," he said handing me the blunt. I rolled my eyes and hit it once, immediately getting choked up forgetting I was a lightweight and shouldn't even be smoking this early. I planned on getting

drunk true enough but getting high would have me somewhere around here stuck. Weed was the only thing that did that to me.

"Now come in here with me baby. Let me taste that pussy," he said pressing his cold Hennessy-filled breath on my neck. I was always weak when it came to this nigga, and I hated it. He had a dick the size of a baby's leg, so I didn't mind the quick sex. He always made sure I got mine and was the first person to show me what an orgasm was.

We started tonguing each other down until I pulled away from his lips.

" Deion, for real baby, why you wanna do this to me? Just let me finish this cheese dip so everything can be done." I begged as he lifted my dress and started rubbing my pussy right there. It was a house full of people and he had his hand on my pussy, not giving a fuck about who could walk in at any moment. He knew just the right things to do to get me in the mood. That sneaky freaky shit always made me super wet. I'd been like that since I was younger. I loved a thrill.

"Come on nigga and only five minutes," I said covering the melting cheese and ground beef up with the lid.

"Yo I'll be back!" he yelled to his homeboys outside who were playing cards, being loud and ignorant as usual. I figured I would take him to the restroom and make him nut fast so I could focus on what was most important today. My baby's party wasn't going to set itself up.

We went inside the restroom nearest to the kitchen and he wasted no time turning me around to lick all in my ass. Deion had been eating my booty way before Kevin Gates made it okay and he loved the taste of my sweet ass.

I grabbed the counter and bit my bottom lip as tightly as I could trying to keep from screaming out his name the way he was swirling his tongue on my ass hope. He was licking and biting my cheeks, smacking them, and making me flinch.

"Oh my god, baby."

"Mmhmm turn your ass around," he said as I turned to face him and jumped on the counter. I knocked hairspray and toothbrushes onto the floor, but I didn't give a fuck at the moment. As long as my pussy was getting ate, I wasn't concerned about shit or anything going on outside of this restroom.

He started to lick up my pussy slowly, making it feel like his tongue was a long snake sliding in between my pussy lips. He immediately started to suck my clit and baby, it felt better than any finger I ever pressed against it.

I grabbed the top of his head and held onto his fresh fade, which was part of the reason I was even in here. Deion always knew how to work his mouth and didn't mind doing it.

"Coco, you in here?" my little brother, Corey, asked banging on the restroom door.

"Yes, what you want nigga?"

"Treasure outside looking for you."

Before I could tell Deion to stop, he was up wiping his mouth and grabbing the doorknob. I couldn't help but notice how quick he was to get out to Miss Treasure after being so "hungry for my pussy." He must've been excited to see her perfect ass, me on the other hand not so much. I had to watch everybody kiss her ass at her competition, now I was going to have to do it again today.

I loved Treasure true enough, but I could never stand her mama and knew my aunt thought so little of me. She never wanted Treasure to come to none of my parties or do anything with me even though we both were the same age. If my mom had power of attorney over all of Grandad's life insurance money from my grandma, we would be set too. Instead, we were left broke while they bought a house and made Treasure a beauty queen.

She was sweet but it was always something about her that told me she had a wild side. She could fool the world and the judges but not me. I couldn't wait until Lisa found out her daughter was not so perfect after all. I would laugh right in her face when she did; I couldn't stand my auntie.

I left out of the restroom and put on the fake act I did with her.

"Cousin! I'm so happy you showed up." I said giving Treasure a long hug. She had on her sash and crown as I asked, and her hair and makeup were flawless of course.

"Where's Chris? I was sure he would be coming with you over here. You know Aunt Lisa thinks we live in the worst neighborhood?" I asked about the perfect-ass doctor boyfriend we met at Aunt Hellen's funeral.

"Oh, he's at home girl. He had a long night at the hospital so I told him I would be fine coming alone," she said smiling and being all pleasant. She had on an all-white dress that stopped above her knee and white heels that had to be 6 inches high. I wanted her to dress up but damn, she was pageant ready out here. She made me feel ugly at my own baby's party.

"Girl, I would take Deion being tired from the hospital any day over a long night in the studio. He still thinks he's going to be a rapper," I said rolling my eyes, making lite of my baby daddy's dead-beat ways. We made our way to the backyard where I had Dream's party halfway set up and the crowd of gatherers had already piled up. A few balloons were floating in the air and I'd even made a balloon arch from a kit I got on Amazon that I attached to the fence. I'd gotten a banner made from a girl on Facebook that said, Treasure the Princess which hung on the back fence, and several other things to bring the theme together. I didn't have much money to work with, but I made do.

"Aww this is so cute Coco. You guys are making me blush with all this stuff. This is really a Treasure-themed party," she said looking at pictures on the candy table. I hated the way my baby looked up to her because she should've looked at me that way. I was the one taking care of her. However, I knew my baby didn't know any better and was just falling into the hype. All little girls loved princesses and Treasure just happened to dress like one; Dream just didn't know this bitch was far from it.

"Yeah girl, Dream loves your ass. She's been asking when you were coming all day. Here she is right here," I said as Dream ran up to us already filthy. As she hugged all on Treasure, I looked around and noticed Deion had disappeared. Soon enough he was coming back out of the house in a change of clothes.

This nigga had on a full unit now and a new pair of shoes that I hadn't ever seen before. I guess this nigga was trying to impress Miss Georgia. All I usually got at the house was gym shorts and a white muscle shirt.

"Hey Deion, it's been a long time," Treasure said giving him a long hug as she held Dream in one arm. I was staring a hole in the back of this nigga's head wondering when he was going to let the bitch go.

"Deion, when are you going to get the cake?" I asked interrupting his clear infatuation with my cousin. I knew he thought she was pretty because he always referred to her as my 'pretty, prissy ass, cousin' when he brought her up. I'd even caught him looking at her Instagram one night he thought I was sleep and liking pictures and shit. I didn't make a big deal because looking is all he better do.

"Don't worry about the cake Coco. Her God daddy, Kaine, going to pick it up for me. You know my nigga got my back," Deion said grabbing me by the waist while bringing up a name that alone sent shivers up my spine.

"Oh, Kaine's coming?" I asked getting all perked up and just as excited to see Kaine as he had been to see Treasure. My crush on Kaine wasn't innocent at all and Kaine could say I'd done everything to him in bed that I'd done to Deion. It didn't make any sense to be that fine, that laid back and respected all over the hood. I knew the day I met that nigga he was going to get me in trouble. I'll never forget how fine he was to me when I first laid eyes on him.

Kaine had moved into town about two years ago from Savannah and was instantly running shit out here. He said he needed a new scene after some girl falsely accused him of rape and got him sent away for four years. The girl's father was the prosecutor in the neighboring county and got DNA planted so that he would be accused of other rapes that happened in the city. They tried to send him away forever even though he was an innocent man. Once the girl's conscience began eating her up she confessed to a roommate and the roommate told the authorities. Kaine was then released from prison and got a settlement from the state too.

Of course, he started flipping it in the streets and bought a studio down here in Atlanta a couple of years ago. He made plenty of money off fools like Deion and was on every girl's wish list, including mine. It was just fucked up because he was cool with my baby daddy. Having him for that one night was enough for me, so I kept it on the hush just in case I wanted to double back one day. That was no lie, the best sex I'd ever had before in my life.

The night Kaine and I fucked, I'd showed up to the studio thinking Deion was there. Kaine said he had gone to north Atlanta with a friend to get a pack of loud and should be back in an hour. I told him I was going to wait for his return, and he shrugged his shoulders like he didn't care. He wasn't checking for me until I walked in front of his chair and sat on his lap. That's when I felt his dick through his pants and dropped to my knees to eat that man up.

"Yes baby, Kaine is coming with the cake don't worry. You know I made him her God Daddy for a reason. You know the original one got killed." He referred to his cousin.

"Yeah, I know. When is he coming though? The party is technically happening right now"

"He said he was on his way to the bakery now and then he will be here in a minute. Chill out," he assured me.

"Well I'm about to go finish up the food, it will never get done if I don't get in here on it."

"I'll come help you, cousin," Treasure said as we walked away.

"Baby, you want me to start the wieners on the pit?"

"Duh, people are about to start showing up since it's time for the party. The people who were actually invited," I said making Treasure laugh at my shade toward all the extras in the backyard.

I felt nothing but eyes watching us as we walked into the house. One set of eyes belonged to Deion, and I knew who they were following. Let me find out he couldn't be trusted with Treasure around. I hope I didn't have to turn this bitch out because he wanted to play, in my face with little Mrs. Perfect.

Chapter 3

Kaine

3:30 pm

"You called me over here just to run?"

"I'm sorry, I'm sorry." Shay adjusted herself on her knees and I slid my dick back inside her. I know I had a lot to take, but I hated when bitches ran from me. My biggest question is why beg for it in the first place if long strokes scare you? I had a bunch of shit to do today, and I fit this hoe in my schedule. This was starting to look like a waste of time.

Her pussy was wet as fuck, I couldn't take that from her. I got it that way rubbing her clit as I stroked her from the back. She was fine with it until I showed her how deep I could go and then she turned into Shacarri Richardson.

I knew I needed to go soon so I held her hips tightly to lock her in place and gave her about twenty deep strokes before she was squirting on her sofa. I admired her body shaking as I shot a load on her ass. I loved when I made bitches lose themselves.

"Fuck Daddy." She collapsed on her stomach shivering as if she was cold. She wasn't though, it was that dick that was cold. I prided myself in a lot of things and slanging priceless dick was one of them.

"You about to roll?"

"Yeah, I told you I had to go do some shit. I'll holler at you later." I turned to walk to the door.

"Wait, let me kiss him goodbye." She smiled brightly, and I allowed her to pull my dick out one more time. I looked down as she kissed my dick and licked it one last time. Just as I was about to put it up, the locks started turning on her door.

"Who is that?" I asked as terror covered her face.

"It's probably my nigga, you gotta go hide on the patio." She tried to direct me out the glass door.

"Hold up. I'm not hiding on the patio. Who the fuck do you think I am?" I looked her up and down.

"You better deal with him the best way you know how," I replied and she hurried to the door and started explaining herself.

"What you pushing me out for, Shay?"

"Baby, I'm so sorry. I didn't know you were getting off this early!" They wrestled at the door.

"Who up in here Shay! Huh? Tell me!"

"Baby I can explain, just let me explain." I met eyes with her nigga. He was in work boots and dirty ass jeans which means she really didn't deserve this nigga. He was out getting dirty to take care of her and she here running from my dick. These Atlanta hoes are really sad.

"I'm going to kill you nigga. You in here fuckin my wife!" He came towards me only stopping when I held my gun up to his face.

"I've killed niggas for less. You may want to find something safe to do."

"Or what, nigga!"

"You won't survive. So, tell me if you are ready to die over this bitch." I replied, and I could see in his eyes that he was standing down. He went back to arguing with his bitch and I walked out the front door without a care in the world. I needed to cross this hoe off the list of bitches I gave dick to. I didn't do messy shit because that would just end me up back in prison.

I had this little party to go to and somehow got volunteered to pick up the cake. I put the address into my GPS and pulled up outside the bakery within twelve minutes. While still outside, I texted this old school nigga about my two grand. I loaned out so much money I had to make a list to keep up with who owed me. I however got back ten percent interest every time so in hindsight it was just another business.

When I walked into the bakery, the door chimed and the lady behind the counter wiped her hands on her apron before picking up a clipboard.

"You here for a pickup baby?"

"Yes ma'am."

"What's the name sweetie?"

"Coco, or Deion," I replied.

"Oh yes, I see. The ten-inch princess cake. I'll grab it from the back." She told me and I waited patiently for her to return. My phone chimed and it was a text message that didn't do shit but piss me off.

I don't have it right now, but I'll have it in a few days. That's a promise, just work with me."

Squirrel sent back giving the wrong answer.

"Okay, this will be $65, sir."

She said, and I took out my wallet. I gave the lady $80 and told her to keep the change. I would just add this to the long bill Deion owes already. He was in so much debt with me he had to do what I asked. If I told him to kill a nigga, he better be pulling the trigger by the same business day.

After I grabbed the cake, I got in my car and drove to Zone One to Vine City where the party was and where that nigga Squirrel hung out. I rode around several blocks until I spotted him standing on the corner next to a bus stop. He tried to act like he didn't see me before I rolled my window down.

"Squirrel, come take a ride with me!" I got

his attention, and he ran up to the car trying to

explain himself.

"What up Kaine. I'm going to have your

money bro I swear, I just need a little more

time-"

"Just get in." I interrupted, making him

climb in my car. This nigga smelled like beer

and filth which pissed me off even more.

"I thought I told you I don't give extensions

on my money?"

"I know it's been three months, but I have

been fucked up. Please believe me bruh, I'm

paying you next week when my mama gets her

disability check." He pleaded as I drove fast as

fuck through the hood.

"Next week seems too far away. I want my money now. So do you, have it?" I placed my gun in my lap. Cars kept turning out in front of me and I had to honk my horn every five seconds.

"I'll pay you back next week Kaine I swear to God. If I have to run into a bank with a pistol to get your money I will. That's on my niece." He said with confidence just making his situation worse. I grabbed his collar with my right hand.

"Don't bring her up nigga. She don't have shit to do with this. She's dead and you're going to let her rest in peace." I hated when people brought up my ex, especially in situations like this. He thought because he was her uncle that it exempted him from my wrath but she wasn't here anymore. That made me angry, and I really didn't have shit to lose. Next time I go to jail it will be for something I really did instead of that fake shit that took so much time of my life. Yeah, it made me a millionaire but it also made me more angry. More cutthroat than before.

I waited until I hit a side street and then I slammed my foot on my break.

"Get the fuck out nigga."

"Thank you, man, thank you. I will pay you back I promise. I swear to you." He got out of the car jogging away. I let him take a few steps before I stuck my pistol out the window and shot him four times in the back.

"Too late nigga." I said before I screeched off.

He couldn't have possibly thought I was letting that shit slide any longer. Now on to this party a few blocks over. I truly had to balance out the bad in my life with the good or I would really be cold-hearted.

Chapter 4

Treasure

4:32 pm

Leave it up to black people to not have their party together on time. I'd heard gunshots that seemed to only be a block away about ten minutes ago, so I was a little skittish. It was about to be 5:00 and we were just getting the food set up under the tent. The cake was still on the way here and there were more grown people in attendance than kids.

I should've known anything given in the hood wouldn't be organized. Coco had a year to plan this baby's party and was still somehow running late. Right now, she only seemed to be concerned with the margarita machine more than anything else and I had done most of the work in the kitchen. I was damn near sweating at an event I was just supposed to appear at. So safe to say I was a little frustrated

Several men had tried to talk to me and if one more nigga called me shawty, I swear I would scream. This was not the type of hood niggas I fantasized about before meeting Chris. I liked a clean-cut man with assets. Dirty and raggedy just didn't do it for me.

I tried to make myself look busy to avoid conversation, but my uncle came scooting his feet towards me anyway with another cigarette in his hand.

"So, tell me again who your mama is? You got to excuse me, I'm a little old. I forget things easily."

"Her name is Lisa Uncle Johnny," I said for the fifteenth time today.

He was full of Bud Light Platinums and asked me who I was every five minutes. Uncle Johnny hadn't been the only one sparking up pointless conversations because Deion was doing it too. He's given me a weird vibe ever since I got here and was constantly following me around. He was seeming to be more helpful to me than Coco, who'd called his name several times. I felt like I was on a stripper pole the way I was being watched by him and I didn't like it. However, I tried to push through for my favorite cousin.

Chris was currently blowing up my phone wanting to know where I was. He was still trying to keep tabs on me as if I hadn't broken things off with him. When he would ask me questions around the house, I acted like I didn't even speak English. His presence was the big push to get me to this party today. I didn't feel like being around him and his child. Coco had him to thank for me standing up in these heels stirring cheese dip.

As a matter of fact, I needed to get out of these heels and grab some flats from the car since I apparently came here to work. I could at least be comfortable while I was uncomfortable at this damn party.

I slipped out the front door before another dude could come up in my face and try to make conversation. Every last one of these niggas over here probably had enough baby mamas to start a cult. That however didn't stop them from trying to talk to me and calling me queen and other dumb shit they figured would impress me. This was one of the downsides of hood men; they didn't know how to romance you and talk to you on some Tevin Campbell type shit. They just called you things like the color you were wearing and tell you how fat your ass was when you walked away.

I went outside and decided to call my mom back now that I was away from the crowd. She definitely couldn't know I was at Coco's house because she would have a fit now that I was officially Miss Georgia.

I knew Facebook would eventually tell her I was here, but I would rather deal with her mouth later than have her yelling in my ear at this damn party. I was already past annoyed, and she wouldn't understand I needed to get away from Chris today. I hadn't even broken it to her about the baby or the blackmail.

I walked down the sidewalk toward the car as the music faded and the phone rang in my ear. That's when I noticed a taller man grabbing a cake out of his car with gold frames on and the whitest pair of Jays I'd seen today. He was about 6'1 with chocolate skin, freshly cut hair, and a low-cut beard. His clothes looked expensive and so did his necklace, which was blinding me from here.

Damn.

I tried to figure out who this was and that's when it dawned on me that he was Dream's God daddy, Kaine.

"Treasure?" my mom said, reminding me I had dialed her number.

"Hey mama, you called me earlier? I'm sorry I didn't answer, I was busy in the kitchen," I said walking closer to Kaine. He was standing outside his car adjusting his necklace after setting the cake on the hood. As I passed by his car, he was looking over his shoulder and we locked eyes. He smirked at me and fine wasn't the word. This man was gorgeous.

After smirking, he licked his lips, and I watched over my shoulder trying to walk as carefully as possible. My mom was talking in my ear, but I wasn't paying her much attention. I honestly wanted him to say something to me but all he'd done was look. That made him even sexier. This man didn't whistle or call me a white dress, he just looked into my eyes.

"Where are you at Treasure? I know you hear me. Your grandfather isn't feeling well again. We're about to go to the E.R.," my mom spoke trying to get my attention. I suddenly tripped over a hole in the sidewalk and stumbled onto my car jamming my finger.

He looked in my direction.

"You iight?" He asked.

I put the phone on mute ignoring my mom because I wasn't going to lose this time to talk to him, especially with a smile like his. I appreciated chocolate men with white teeth. Chris was the same way, only Kaine had diamonds across the bottom of his, which looked even better if you ask me.

"Yes, I'm fine. I just need to get out of these shoes," I said nervously feeling a bit shy talking to him. I talked to plenty of people daily in the pageant world, but still. None made me feel like this.

"Yeah, you wild for rocking them shoes out here. Isn't this a kid's party?" He chuckled after grabbing the cake.

"Yeah, I'm crazy for wearing this but I'm a girly girl. I'm guessing you're here for the party as well? You're Dream's God daddy, Deion's friend, right?"

"Yeah, but I wouldn't say friend. That's my homie though."

"Why is the friend title out of the question?"

"Cause that nigga wild. How do you know him?" He asked, and my mama interrupted, yelling in my ear.

"Treasure! Do you hear me? I'm starting to think you're not okay. Is something going on with you?" my mom questioned through the phone.

"No, mama, I'm good. I'm just about to walk into the gym. I had way too much sushi last night and wanna work off every pound." I fabricated grabbing my sandals from the trunk.

"Oh, well yes, I'll be at the hospital probably all night. Just when I thought I had a chance to rest after the Miss Georgia pageant.

"Okay, and I'm praying for Granddad and call me if I need to come up there, you know how I feel about my pappy."

"Okay, baby I will. Be careful and remember to have Chris go anywhere with you tonight if you leave the house. Don't be traveling by yourself at night Treasure.

"I won't Mom."

"Okay, love you."

"Love you too," I said getting off the phone in a rush to get back to the party. I was just ready to leave ten minutes ago but now I could get a few more glances at Kaine's fine ass before leaving.

I made my way back into the backyard and approached Coco and Deion, standing there talking to him. I took the opportunity to walk into the conversation and everyone stopped talking when I strolled up.

"Kaine this is my cousin Treasure, Treasure this is Kaine," Coco said as he extended his hand out to shake mine.

"Yeah, I met her out by the street. This is the famous Miss Georgia, right?"

"Yes, nice to formally meet you," I responded holding on to his smooth hand connected to his diamond-draped wrist.

"Likewise. Congratulations on your well-deserved win." He never stopped making eye contact with me.

"Well deserved, that's nice of you to say. Do you keep up with the pageant world?".

"Nah, but I can tell just by looking at you that it was over before it started. You pretty as a mutha fucka and pretty bitches always winning that type of shit," he called me bitch in mid-sentence as if it was nothing. It really didn't come off as offensive though because of how smooth he spoke. His demeanor and attitude were sexy as hell and the ruggedness just added something different. If this had been another man, I would've checked him for calling me a bitch, but Kaine didn't look like he could be checked anyway.

Now that I was directly in front of him, I saw that he smelled good, and it was refreshing with all the sweaty musk out here. Kaine didn't smell like cheap cologne either and it had to be something expensive because my nose wasn't itching. I felt like I knew the smell, I just couldn't put my finger on it. I was more than intrigued so I had to ask.

"Kaine, what kind of cologne do you have on?"

"None," he looked me in my eyes and then kept scanning the crowd.

"Are you sure? I feel like I know that scent from somewhere."

"Yeah, I'm sure. Are you telling me I'm lying, Treasure?" he asked, this time giving me a quick smile to show he was joking.

"I'm not saying that at all. I mean, whatever scent you have on is nice. I, I just felt like I recognized it," I said stuttering over my words.

"Thanks, but nah, I don't wear cologne. It may be my body wash or laundry detergent."

"Really, that's it?"

"Yeah, you can come back to my crib to see what I mean if you don't believe me," he said licking his lips making Deion and Coco laugh as they watched our back and forth.

"Treasure, Kaine's ex-boo was a pageant girl too,"

"Oh really, what did she win?" I asked knowing I didn't care about all these local ass pageant girls around Atlanta. I knew when they had a Miss Twerk some pageant that they were just giving sashes to anybody.

"She was Miss something. I don't know, I wasn't into that shit like that. Somebody killed her though. You better watch yourself. This is an evil world we live in. Pretty bitches getting whacked too," he said looking toward the ground as if this conversation was starting to make him uncomfortable. I had knots in my stomach hearing his ex was a former pageant girl. He had to be talking about the same girl who was the reason I was standing in this sash today. The same girl my mother and my boyfriend plotted to kill so that I could become Miss Decatur.

"I'm sorry to hear about your ex. What was her name if you don't mind me asking? Maybe I know of her," I asked hoping he would actually say someone else.

"Her name was Jalani. She died about a year ago."

He replied, and I was legit lost for words. Things between us just became a little awkward but that still didn't take away the fact that he was fine. Jalani had good taste in men.

Chapter 5

Coco

The disrespect and jealousy I felt were at an all-time high. Every man here was checking for Treasure including mine, and I had something for his ass, especially after she leaves. Deion was so infatuated with the girl he was in her face every five minutes telling her how 'proud' of her he was and how happy he was to see her win. Those were words he never said to me even on my best days when appreciation would've gone a long way. I've braided five heads in one day just to keep the lights on and all he could do was complain about how I hadn't cooked that day. Just because I didn't support them stupid-ass rap dreams of his, he felt as if he didn't have to support my reachable goals.

All I ever wanted was to be loved and good enough, but it seemed like I was constantly fighting and trying to prove myself to him and everybody else around me. My mom didn't think I would ever be about shit because she wasn't, and she wanted me stuck with her forever. I loved her to death, but I wanted more than this. I needed more than just my good looks like Treasure.

I'd been paying attention to her too. She loved the attention she'd been getting today, and she was also in Kaine's face this entire time. She was small-talking him to death and he was flirting right back, which was making me just as jealous as if it were Deion. No, he wasn't my man, but I'd called dibs on him a long time ago. Maybe I should tell her so she could get out his face and go home to Carlton Banks or whatever her doctor nigga's name was.

"Yo Treasure, what you know about that Isley brothers?" Deion asked Treasure when he noticed her bobbing her head to the music. Everyone was out here jamming but he just had to put his attention on her finding any way to make small talk. This shit was making me more and more aggravated as time went on. I didn't know I had a baby by a dick rider. I thought I was supposed to be the one riding the dick.

"Deion, I'm no unseasoned chicken now, I told you that. I may be pretty, but I'm still hood at heart," she said batting her hazel eyes, which most likely came from her rapist father.

"The Hood Mona Lisa, huh?" Kaine said, puffing on a big ass blunt, breaking his usual silence.

"Yeah, the hood Mona Lisa, I like that,"
Treasure said giving Kaine a smirk as he licked
his lips looking away with his gangsta ass.
He normally never said much when he was
around and usually let Deion run his mouth
while he sat back and laughed. He'd talked more
today than any day he's been around, so I know
he must've been feeling Treasure. He was gazing
at the bitch like she was the Mona Lisa painting.
That was the same look that had me bent over
the top of his studio equipment.

"Treasure, I wanna take a picture with you by my new car that Uncle Kaine got me," Dream said coming up to Treasure and climbing in her lap. Treasure was in the middle of taking a sip of water and Dream knocked the bottle from her mouth spilling it all over Treasure's white dress.

"Oh my god Dream, you gotta watch yourself, baby," I said not getting a chance to jump up before Deion and Kaine were both coming to her rescue. Kaine grabbed Dream and started to tickle her as Deion sprinted into the kitchen saying he would get a towel. I hadn't seen him move that quickly since the bounty hunter came to get him from jumping bond. I wish they would show up right now and take his thirsty ass to jail.

"Cousin, I'm so sorry, I don't know why she does that. She has no regard for other people's space."

"It's okay girl, at least it's white and it was water."

"Yes, girl but you can see your see your boobs," I said intentionally trying to make her feel uncomfortable.

That instead made Kaine's attention go back to her and he said," "Damn." Raising his eyebrow then giving Treasure a look as if he wanted to lick her right here.

"Here you go, you can use this," he said giving her the white towel he kept in the back pocket of his shorts. He was a street nigga through and through, so he always kept a rag on him, preferably on the right side of his back pocket. Him giving her his towel was like a nigga letting a female wear his letterman in high school, niggas weren't doing that for just anybody.

Who was I kidding though? His old bitch was supposedly into that pageant bullshit, so maybe that's why he was checking for Treasure. Either way, I was salty as hell and feeling some type of way.

"Treasure let me go see if I have another dress for you to put on, you're soaked."

"No, it's okay l. I think I should just go anyway. I have to get up super early to work out with my trainer. I really should be leaving,"

"Aww, babe you sure? It's no problem, I can go get you a dress now out of my closet. If it wasn't her birthday, I would whoop her butt. I'm sorry she did that," I said sticking my lip out as if I was really sorry or disappointed. I was honestly happy she was leaving because I was tired of seeing niggas drool over her. I was the grand dame of this block. Treasure needed to go back to the pageant world where she belonged because this was my stage. I could see after today she just wasn't for me anymore; her being in my territory wasn't working and she needed to go back to Buckhead, period.

"I thought you were about to be my spades partner," Kaine said to Treasure seemingly reflecting on one of the side conversations they'd had tonight.

"I told you I used to play well back in the day. I don't know about now," Treasure moved her hair to the side, flirting with Kaine.

"Well, I wanna see what you working with. Coco go ahead and get her a change of clothes before I have to slap one of these niggas for trying to look at her chest." He added, and I'm sure smoke was coming out of my ears.

"Looking at my chest like you are?" She smiled like it was cute. This girl was such a hoe. Miss Georgia my ass.

"I can't help it. They perfect. Shid, you're

perfect." Kaine said to Treasure, making me

need a Xanax to calm myself down. How the

hell did he figure she was perfect when he'd only

known her for a couple of hours? Let me get

away from this shit because I couldn't stand it

anymore. He was being mad disrespectful at

this point, and I would look wild as

hell snapping at him for getting at my cousin.

I went into the house and found Deion in

the linen closet going through dirty ass towels,

being little to no help as usual.

"Damn, all these towels look like worn-out

granny panties."

"Well, buy some more towels since you got a problem," I said taking a towel from his hand and throwing it to the ground.

"Man, you need to find that girl something to wipe up with. You can't just leave her like that."

"Don't worry about a towel. Kaine gave her a towel and I'm getting her a dress," I said going into my closet looking for the least seductive thing I could find.

"Well, I'm about to go back out there. You ready to start drinking this margarita shit?" he questioned as I ignored him and continued to look through the racks. Disappointed in him wasn't the word because now I see that he can be attentive, he was just lazy with me.

It's crazy how men could be what they wanted for who they wanted and would wait hand and foot for the next bitch. He better beat his meat for days after this party because that's the only way he was going to get a nut off anytime soon. Club Coco was closed for business, so I hope he licked his lips good after he ate my ass. That will be the closest memory he will have of my box for a while.

"What's wrong with you Coco?"

"Nothing."

"Come on now, I know when you pissed off so what's up? Did your period shit start? Don't tell me you're about to be bitching for days," he said shaking his head while still lingering around our bedroom door.

"No, I'm not on my period, and why are you worried about me anyway? Go see if Treasure is on her cycle since you wanna know everything about her ass."

"Man, you can't be serious Coco." He laughed in my face.

"Oh yes, I am so get out of my face with that stupid ass laughing. I'm not in the mood." I rolled my eyes at him.

Deion was known for trying to laugh situations off when he knew he was in the wrong. Clown niggas always doing clown shit and our relationship was a circus because of him.

"So, just because I'm nice to your kinfolk you think I want her?"

"Nice to her and clearly wanting to fuck are two different things. You just don't know how it makes me feel to see you treat another female how I want to be treated,"

"Dang man, I'm sorry you feel like that shawty, for real. I was just trying to be a good host," he said pausing as if he was thinking of what to say.

"What do you want me to do to make it up to you? Eat your pussy or something? Just let me know." he said making me smack my lips.

"Deion get out of my face."

"Baby, I'm sorry. Damn." He wrestled with me to hug me around my waist.

"Why are you letting your cousin get to you like that? I thought y'all was cool, twin cousins and shit," he said asking the same question I'd been asking myself all day. I was always a little jealous of her but now I seemed to be growing hate in my heart for Treasure. I honestly wish I would've never invited her here no matter what Dream wanted. A lifelong bond was being ruined because I couldn't stand to see the love she received. Her life was turning out to be perfect and mine was not.

"I don't know why; I just hate how perfect she puts on to be. Like she's so fucking good and does no wrong."

"Oh, so you think she putting on?"

"Yeah, nobody's that good that came from this hood. I don't care how long she's been away, she's still an East Atlanta girl at heart just like me. I know she has secrets that just haven't been exposed yet.

"Well make her expose herself. If you can't figure her out, then make her lay out the blueprint for you."

"How am I supposed to do that? Make her take a lie detector test in front of the whole world?" I asked responding to his dumb-ass advice.

"Make her expose herself without even knowing she's telling her secrets. Put some of these bitches in her drink or some shit. Nobody can keep a lie going when they high as flight attendant pussy," Deion said going into his top drawer and pulling out a pill bottle full of Xanax fresh from a re-up. Because he wasn't making money off his music, he sold drugs part time too.

"Deion, she is not going to take a pill."

"She ain't gotta know she's taking it. Just slide it in a drink," he said handing me the bottle. I immediately opened it and took one, dry swallowing it, putting a horrible taste in my mouth. I promised myself this morning I wouldn't pop a pill today, but the stress of a kid's party made me wanna be out of my mind and away from reality. This was no different than a white bitch named Karen taking one after a long day of soccer practice. Though it seemed odd for Deion to think of giving her one of these, I was seriously considering it just to see the real her.

"Deion, give me that book right there to crush this up, and this is between you and me, okay? Don't judge me, I just wanna prove a point," I said already feeling the guilt as I put the plan into motion.

He handed me the book and put the pill bottle back into the dresser. I was so nervous I was shaking but this shit had to be done.

"Deion, one more thing."

"What baby?" he responded as he stood near the door getting ready to leave.

"Don't make me put something in your drink that will have you cold by tomorrow morning."

"I hear your crazy ass." He laughed brushing it off as he left out of the door. He took me as a joke, but I was serious. That bitch could have everything under the sun except him or Kaine for that matter. She would probably never give them a chance anyway. Deep down inside, I know she thought she was better than all of us. She just played nice.

Chapter 6

Treasure

I was sweaty as hell and still in Coco's backyard by nightfall. I originally planned to be at my mom's house by now curled up on her couch. I made up my mind a little earlier that I wasn't going back home so even being in the hood was better than my apartment. Plus, I was actually having fun. The music was bussing, and I was in the company of a cute guy who was attracting me just by not being thirsty. If anything, I was the one being thirsty, lingering around him and making small conversation. He was a mystery for sure and I wanted to know more about him.

My people in the hood had high expectations of me, and I always tried to live up to them. I hid things I knew would disappoint them or just flat-out embarrass me. I would never tell Coco that my perfect boyfriend stepped out and had a baby on me. She always said we were

the perfect couple along with everyone else in the world. Now I don't know how much longer I could hide that we weren't together or how I no longer wanted to. Shoot, my eyes were already wandering elsewhere. Every five seconds I was looking at Kaine.

"Can I help you with something?" I flirted with Kaine who I caught looking my way.

"What do you mean?"

"You keep looking at me."

"How you know I wasn't looking past you?" I shrugged my shoulders and he laughed.

"Ohhhhh, I get it. You are used to niggas staring at you, but I swear I was just looking at the kids," he said leaning back into his chair and pulling out his phone. Normally this type of rejection from a man would bother me but I liked this shit. Kaine was a code I would have to crack and for the first time, I would have to work for someone's attention.

"Here cousin, take a shot with me. Remember you promised you would when you first got here!" Coco said walking under the tent to hand me a plastic shot glass.

"Come on Treasure, just take one with me. We've never gotten drunk together legally. Remember when we pretended that we were drunk off that Sparkling water at Kassidy's wedding? Come on just do it this one time. Who knows when we will see each other again?" she said putting peer pressure on me. I agreed to take the shot to hush her up and not look like a snob in front of Kaine.

I took the shot dropping some on my already damp dress. Thank God I had this blue Jean jacket on from Coco.

"Yuck! What is that? Gross!" I said making the ugliest face from the bitterness of that shot.

"Lightweight." Kaine laughed and shook his head.

"Well, are you taking a shot?" I asked Kaine.

"Nah I'm good, I don't drink," he responded, showing me yet again that he was different in this yard of dogs. Every other man here has been drunk since before the sun went down and on some type of drugs. I could appreciate a man who could say no as I did most of my life. The only time I honestly drank was when I was out of pageant season or when I was stressed. This time I was both, so I fell into Coco's pressure easily.

"That's good. Drinking is bad for you."

"I smoke though, I'm sure you don't. Your lips still pink."

"You're right, I don't." I smiled bashfully.

Our conversation was interrupted by commotion in the house and glass shattering out the kitchen window. Everyone started looking toward the back door and we all stood up to see what was going on.

Coco and Deion made their way to the house and started yelling at someone about tearing up their shit. Moments later you could hear Coco screaming for everyone to get out of her house and that the party was over.

"Well, I guess that's my cue to leave, I need to change anyway," I said to Kaine who was standing right beside me. I may be making this up, but I swear he was turned to my body as if he were protecting me.

"I don't think she talking to us. She talking to them niggas in there tripping. Just follow me through the front door and we can keep kicking it here." he said making me feel quite comfortable in the chaos.

At that moment, I got a phone call from Chris again and I hit deny so quickly he probably thought my phone was dead. He could sit at home and play daddy by himself because I was out mingling.

That shot already had me feeling a way and so did Kaine grabbing me by the wrist and leading me around the house. If aphrodisiac was a person, it would be him because he legit made me want to have sex. Kaine was tall, chocolate, and protective so I could never get enough of his presence. I wasn't leaving just yet. I needed to have a little more fun before I left.

Chapter 7

Kaine

2 hours later

When I walked into the kitchen to grab a water. Coco was sitting on her washing machine smoking a blunt.

"Hey, you, I'm about to come back in there." Her head bobbled like it was too heavy for her neck. I didn't respond and she still felt the need to keep talking.

"You know we can't smoke around Hillary Banks so you can come in here if you need to hit something."

"No thanks, I'm straight," I replied, walking out of the kitchen. Another lil shawty I'd been fucking with hit me up about coming through my house tonight, but I told her no too. I tried to not fuck any of these bitches too many times because that's when real feelings get involved. I wasn't emotionally available to anybody. I'd maybe slept with five girls this year and it was already summer.

I tried to be careful with hoes and only sleep with ones I could somewhat trust. After spending three years in prison because a bitch lied about me raping her, I vowed to never go back because of a spiteful bitch again. I spent my 21st birthday behind bars instead of in between something wet because I didn't want that bitch no more. Everything happened for a reason though, because I got paid and fell for the girl who helped set me free, Jalani. She was roommates with my accuser and spilled the beans after she confessed it all was a setup. Life was good for a while after I got out until Jalani got killed.

I knew with my past there was no way they wouldn't say I took her life, especially with her being who she was in Atlanta. We were already a secret, and I knew people wouldn't believe she could love a gangsta like me. I stayed in my house for days just waiting for them to come get me, but they never showed up. So, I never hit their radar which was a good thing. After all, I was on a flight to California when she got killed anyway.

I hated that my baby had to go out like that, and I know whatever she went through she suffered. Jalani was slaughtered and I always had flashbacks to that night on the plane feeling like something was wrong. I was just with her earlier when a nigga had been following us around the supermarket. When I turned to confront him, he just looked scared and walked away. We figured it was just a fan who wanted to take a picture or something, but I should've stayed in Georgia that night and been there to protect her. I would've died for her because she saved my life. I loved that girl.

Now, most of the time all I did was come to the hood and chill with this nigga Deion at his crib or the studio. He didn't have shit going on in life, but he was funny as hell, and he did lift a nigga spirit from time to time. I'd found ways to deal with losing Jalani, besides doing drugs and alcohol and putting myself in the grave. Yeah, I smoked, but I didn't let grief lead me to fucking my body up with crack or other hard drugs. I manned up and dealt with the hurt every day as my father taught me. I was lonely but I found ways to handle myself.

"Ouu, this is my song." Treasure stood up and plopped back down.

"You slumped Shawty, you might wanna have a seat," Shawty was all of a sudden on her ass. She was putting on good when she first got here, acting like she didn't drink or smoke. After everybody left, she started wilding and letting loose, dancing all over me and shit. If she wasn't clearly out of her mind, I would enjoy it, but I honestly felt sorry for her. Shawty was too full, and her cousin Coco couldn't be any help because she was just as out of her mind.

Coco had grabbed my dick more than once tonight and was real-life tripping. That nigga Deion just didn't know how fucked up Shawty was and how done she was with his shit. She'd told me all that the night I fucked her and told me while I was inside her that I was bigger and better than him.

I didn't let that shit get to my head though, I wasn't even trying to be the type of nigga that fucked behind his homies. Shit happens though and this nigga was foul himself. The only person I felt sorry for in this situation was Dream. She was too pretty to have parents that just didn't give a fuck about each other. They were just together because of her but didn't know they were hurting her in the process.

While sitting on the couch, Coco's brother Lil Corey stuck his head in the door.

"Yo, Kaine, can I talk to you for a minute?" He asked, and I got up to follow him out the door.

"What's up, man?"

"Shid, life really. Did you see my spring game highlights from April?"

"Did I? Man, I was there. You know I wouldn't have missed it. I just had to leave early to handle a little business."

"Yeah, I get it." He dropped his head and kicked in the dirt like he was scared to talk.

"What's up lil nigga? What's going on?" I asked, genuinely concerned about the little dude. Being around Deion I've gotten to know his little brother-in-law pretty well. He was a four-star athlete who could be something if he put his mind to it. I didn't mind talking with him about anything. I knew niggas like Deion didn't have shit positive to add to his life.

"Kaine, I killed someone." He finally spoke up, honestly making my stomach hurt.

"What did you do? When?"

"I shot him, a few days ago. We hit a lick together and he wasn't trying to give me half."

"Damn man. You still got the gun?"

"Yeah, it's in the room. They haven't found his body though. He's behind an abandoned house in zone 3."

"They will find him soon enough," I replied, thinking about what to do.

"Listen, go get the gun and wipe it off good before putting it in my backseat. I'll get rid of it and don't tell anybody what you did alright."

"I won't."

"Alright, make sure it's clean," I replied as he went into the house. Corey was the prime example of kids in the hood who fall victim to their circumstances. This unfortunately won't be his last body. Once you spill someone's blood you won't have a problem doing it again.

Chapter 8

Deion

The house was pretty much clear, and the only people left here were me, my homeboy Kaine, my mother-in-law Mrs. Juanita, Coco, and Treasure's fine ass. We'd sent Dream off with my sister and had drinks and weed floating in the air. I'd had a perc and two cups of Hennessy straight, and too many blunts to count. Coco was stumbling around high as fuck and Treasure was on cloud nine too from the Xanax Coco slipped to her. It was wild that my baby mama did that shit but that's how bitches are with each other. Especially the fine ones. They were both that plus some, and the only difference between the two was that I hadn't had Treasure's pussy yet. I said yes because I planned on trying it out tonight. That's why I convinced Coco to drug her ass.

"Treasure come take another shot with ya boy?"

"No, Deion, I'm done. I told you the last shot was my last one. I'm tapping out." Treasure slurred turning down the 10th shot I offered her. Once the pill kicked in, she had been more relaxed about chilling and drinking with us. My girl may have drugged Shawty but she did help her to have a good time. On top of that, she was about to get some good dick too. I wasn't the longest muthafucka out there, but I knew how to work my shit. I always had Coco and other hoes screaming my name.

"Miss Georgia, you good?" I asked Treasure who was standing in a corner gyrating her body to the music playing from the speaker.

I'd put three more pills in Coco's drink so I could have Treasure's high ass to myself tonight no interruptions. I didn't feel bad about it because I was just reaping the benefits of having a pageant queen in my house tonight. I couldn't wait to tear her ass up.

"Coco you need to go lay your ass down now. You sloppy as hell," I said to my baby mama who was barely coherent.

"Yeah, her too, shawty faded," Kaine said pointing toward Treasure.

"I'm not faded Kaine, what makes you say that?" Treasure slurred with her eyes half closed. Coco mumbled something and then shut her eyes completely, letting me know she was almost passed out. I stood her up and walked her into the room to lay her down as she mumbled some shit about sex. I didn't want her tonight.

When I came back into the living room, Treasure had sat down on the couch next to Kaine and seemed to be just enough out of her mind for me to go in for the kill. I needed to get rid of this nigga so I could take Treasure in the back room to see if she could suck dick like her cousin. I was hyped for this shit. Miss Georgia on my dick.

"Ay man, you about to roll? A nigga ready to lay it down. Smash something real quick," I said to Kaine.

"Nigga it's going to be like you fucking a dead body. Coco had way too much of whatever tonight." Kaine joked as he stood from the couch.

"Yeah, but I'm not worried about Coco. One of these hoes in here is just coherent enough for me to fuck," I replied looking toward Treasure. Her honey-brown legs were exposed and made a nigga want to bite. I wasn't going to just bite them bitches, I was going to lick them too. Treat them like fingertips full of Cheeto dust.

"Man, you wilding, I know you not trying to take lil shawty right here for a ride. You know she is out of her mind too."

"Yeah, so what? She's going to like it once we get started," I said taking another chug from the Hennessy bottle and then walking up to Treasure.

She was leaning back on the couch with her legs crossed toward Kaine. I sat on the other side of her, then wrapped my arm around her waist and rubbed her stomach.

"Uh uh, Deion what are you doing?" Treasure said slurring and moving away slowly. I knew she would act like she didn't want it at first, but eventually, she would let me have my way.

"Yo bro, chill. You know this girl is not in her right mind."

"Man, this hoe has been flirting with me all day. I know she wants this wood," I said rubbing my hand across her soft plump breast. She squirmed at first but eventually stopped resisting my touch and let me have my way.

I thought Kaine would've been walked out the door, but this nigga was still standing here. He must've wanted to two-man this hoe.

"Deion, nigga, your wilding for real. Leave her alone. She clearly maxed out, go fuck yo bitch; she right in the other room," Kaine said aggressively.

"Damn, my nigga, mind your business. You act like this yo bitch or something. Calm down, relax. You stick around long enough, and I'll let you have a piece of her ass too," I said kissing her neck as I began to feel her nipples.

I quickly started kissing my way down her chest and then toward her breast to see how her nipples tasted. I couldn't wait to swirl my tongue around her pussy too.

"Nah bruh, I'm not letting this shit go down like this. You tripping," Kaine said with more hostility in his voice.

"But what's your problem though twin? You know how shit goes over here so don't try and intervene."

"What kind of nigga are you? This girl came over here to host your daughter's birthday party as a favor and now you trying to rape her. You mean to tell me I been around a fuck nigga this long?"

"Rape her?" I questioned and busted out laughing at the irony of this nigga accusing anybody of rape. I know he didn't do the shit, but he was a once-convicted rapist, not me.

"Yeah, rape nigga. If she wanted to fuck you, she would've fucked you sober."

"Man, I'm not trying to hear nothing you talking about. You acting like some type of cop ass nigga right now. I mean I know she had a crown on her head like your old woman but this ain't her. Shid, maybe if you acted like that about her, she wouldn't be dead right now," I said taking a pull from the inch-long blunt burning my lips.

The next thing I knew this nigga Kaine was swinging a right hook so hard he knocked the hearing out of my ear and blood onto the floor. After that hit, several more punches followed, and I couldn't even catch my balance to stand up and fight this nigga back.

"Nigga don't you ever bring her up again! I will kill you nigga! Niggas like you the reason she dead now!" he said hitting me with one last blow. I was leaking from every direction, and I tried to say something to the nigga, but my mouth was so full of blood, all I could do was spit.

"You lucky this girl here and I don't want her wrapped up in a murder charge because I would kill you right now. And that's on my mama and yours nigga." He kicked me one last time.

"Treasure, come with me because this nigga on some hoe shit. Get up, come on. Let me get you home," he said helping Treasure off the couch on some Superman shit. I was sure my nose was broken, and I had a side tooth on the floor.

Had I known this nigga was a pussy, I would've never had him around me in the first place. I'm not a bitch, I don't care about his money.

Chapter 9

Treasure

8:00 am

When I opened my eyes, I can admit I had no idea where I was. The room was dark, and I felt frozen as I laid under the cover. For a moment I was scared to move hoping I wasn't in danger. I tried to think back over everything that took place last night, but I couldn't remember shit.

I know I hadn't been abducted. I mean I'm sure I wouldn't be asleep in a big comfortable bed right now. When I heard dishes rattling in the other room, I decided to get up and see where I was. I tripped over a pair of shoes and damn near broke my knee running into the nearby dresser.

"Shit," I mumbled to myself looking for a light switch to find my purse or the keys to my car. I didn't even see my phone anywhere in sight and I could only imagine the number of calls I'd gotten by now.

I took a deep breath and then opened the door walking into the next room not knowing what to expect. I was taken aback seeing a well-kept living room with beautiful furniture and no one seemingly in sight. I looked around the room and was quite impressed with the beautiful art on the walls and a huge flatscreen mounted near the door. There was only black, white, and gray in here, so I knew it had to be a man's place. A bitch would've added some color by now, especially a bitch like me.

"You finally up, huh? You slept like 10 hours on that shit." I heard a familiar voice say from the kitchen. I looked toward the corner to see Kaine sitting at the kitchen island on a barstool. Once again, I was trapped in the finesse and stature that only a real street dude could carry. He was dressed down but still carried the same swag he had yesterday. The white tee, sky blue gym shorts, and ankle socks made him look just as good as the Jordan's and Gucci shirt did yesterday. Still, even with his appearance, I didn't understand how I got here. I don't remember even getting in this man's car.

"Kaine, did we?"

"Naw, we didn't," he said taking a sip from a coffee mug.

"I don't fuck sloppy bitches," he said pushing the extra cup on the counter towards me.

"Pour some tea. That may help get that shit off your back."

"What shit? I'm confused as to why you keep saying shit. What's going on?" I asked crossing my arms.

"Xanax I'm guessing, and I saved you from getting raped last night. I tried to take you home, but you had no idea where you lived so I brought you here," he said making me immediately feel panic cover my body.

"Xanax! I don't remember taking any pills yesterday! What the hell are you talking about?"

"Yeah, I'm sure you don't remember taking any, but you did." He got up from the barstool and stood over me.

"What did I tell you last night when we first met? Watch yourself. It's an evil world we live in."

"Okay but what do you mean someone was going to rape me? Can you just tell me what happened last night?" I questioned, damn near in tears pleading for answers.

Our conversation was then interrupted by knocking and Kaine walked to the door to see who it was. He opened it and stood in the doorway not letting whomever in.

"Man, why are you back over here? I told you I didn't have shit for you."

"Okay Kaine but why can't you just talk to me? I can't stand you feeling like I played you or did anything on purpose. I really thought she was yours," the girl said as I stood off to the side not wanting to be seen but still eavesdropping on their conversation.

"I don't give a damn what you were trying to do shawty. As far as I'm concerned, you're for the streets now. I don't have shit for you."

"You don't gotta be like that Kaine. Look at you, acting all high and mighty like you're not fucking any and everybody in Atlanta. You probably got somebody here with you right now," she said making me feel a little uneasy as I stayed out of her site.

"And why does it matter what the fuck I'm doing, leave Chanel," he said attempting to close the door before she fought her way into the apartment

"So, this is why you can't hear me out! You got some nerve trying to push me away when you fucking whoever."

"Megan get the fuck out of my house. I'm giving you like five seconds," Kaine said standing in the same spot near the door. The loudmouth hoe was now standing there grimacing at us like a wolf to sheep and I didn't know what was about to happen at this point.

I stared back at her trying not to look as scared, but I'd honestly never fought before.

"Chanel by the time I get to three you dying" Kaine interrupted our stare down and she rolled her eyes and pushed past him. He closed the door and locked both locks, turning to shake his head as if he were over the situation.

"Damn, I see your life is full of drama just like mine. It even comes to your doorstep too" I said as Kaine sat down on his couch.

"My life is usually not. This hoe just got brave is all." He replied grabbing the remote.

"You going to just stand over there or you going to come sit down?" He smiled, and I brushed off the shit that just happened taking a seat.

"So... what were you saying about last night? I don't mean to bug; I'm just trying to figure out what all happened at Coco's house,"

"Just know I saved you and stay away from there. That's no place for a girl like you," he said as he grabbed a lighter and sparked a blunt. He blew a cloud of smoke right in front of him and sat back on the couch like it immediately relaxed him. I usually liked to be miles away from smoke, but I just sat there letting him blow it in front of our faces. The shit was sexy as hell to me.

I leaned back against the couch to relax until I realized I was probably the most wanted girl in America right now. I needed to call my mom before she had me on the news by 5:00. I can see the headline now.

"Can I use your phone? Or do you know where mine is?" I asked and Kaine pointed to the coffee table in front of him. There sat my iPhone 14 shattered across the entire front screen making me sick to my stomach.

"Damn, what happened to it?"

"It fell on the ground when I was carrying you in here last night. You're heavier than you look," he said smirking with his eyes dimmed from the weed. I couldn't get mad at the fact that my phone was cracked because his charming ass had admitted to carrying me in last night. If only I hadn't been so out of my mind, I could've enjoyed the ride. Speaking of ride, damn his lips looked good.

I shook off my hoeish desires and attempted to use my phone. I slid my finger across the screen picking up glass with nothing working. I smacked my lips and immediately panicked seeing I'd missed over 200 calls from my mom, Chris, and many others that I couldn't respond to.

"This phone will not let me unlock it. Can I use your cell?" I asked sitting the phone back down on the table.

"Just use the house phone. It's sitting right there."

"Dang, you still have a house phone?"

"It came with the cable, plus I need a backup in case I ever come home drunk and drop my phone like you did," he made light of my situation. I couldn't do anything but blush feeling as if I was in the presence of some type of celebrity or something.

I knew my mama's number by heart, so I dialed it and prayed she picked up an unknown call.

"Hello, mom."

"Treasure! Are you okay? Baby where are you?" my mom asked in a panic as I suspected she would be.

"Yes, Mom I'm fine. I broke my phone last night. I've been trying to remember your number all night and I just got the right number," I said spilling the lies as they came to my head.

"Oh, my goodness Treasure, thank God. Trisha, it's Treasure on the phone. Tell the officers she said she's fine. Treasure where are you? Chris said you didn't come home, and we've been looking for you all morning."

"I went to Cali's house after I worked out and lost track of time. I didn't want to leave late because of what you told me about being out at night. I didn't know his number to call him either. Plus, we had a small fight, so I didn't want to reach out to him on social media." I added trying to make sense of why I ghosted Chris too.

"My goodness, Treasure, you've given me a heart attack this morning. Please don't ever do this again. Baby call Chris and let him know you're okay, he went out looking for you as soon as I said you weren't here. Let me give you his number so you can call him. He's worried sick Treasure," my mom said as she began to read Chris's number.

"678-7845, Treasure, you there?" she asked as I sat there quietly listening to the number I already knew. Chris was the last person I wanted to call right now.

I guess I could call him and tell him a quick lie to hold him off from his blackmail tour. Today was about me and peace and I didn't need my dumb ass ex still looking for me to get his feelings hurt. As much as I hated it, I had to string him along until I figured out what to do about his snake ass.

Chapter 10

Chris

I have been riding around the city looking for Treasure all day while drinking and trying to cope with all the pressure on me right now. My girl hadn't come home, and my biggest fear had set in, Treasure might actually leave me.

Her mama thought she was somewhere hurt but I knew better. She was just running off because of our problems at home. I know how Treasure thinks, she's calling my bluff because she figured I didn't wanna spend the rest of my life in prison, but I didn't care. I would flip on them and get no time.

My time and energy in this relationship was not going to waste. I was going to be the only nigga posting Miss America in his bed, not anybody else. I wanted to kill over her leaving me. I didn't know what I would do seeing her with somebody else. I knew without her I would really not have anything. She was my last accomplishment and one I couldn't lose.

Atlanta was big and small at the same time. I knew where Treasure hung out and what spots she would never hit. Treasure was usually at one of three places, but I hadn't seen her at either one. She wasn't at the gym, at the mall, and not her mama's house, which would've been my first guess when she didn't come home. I hadn't seen her since yesterday evening, and I knew she probably wouldn't come back if I didn't put my foot down on this Jalani shit. I was going to give her until nightfall before I said fuck it all and turned us in.

I was still looking for my ain't shit baby mama, Megan, and could strangle that bitch for even bringing this on me. I had the baby in the back seat as I drove recklessly through the streets. I had to do everything for her alone because nobody knew I had her. I changed her, fed her, and bathed her. I'd even given her a nickname just to have something to call her when I was trying to calm her down. Her actual name was on the paternity papers, but I couldn't say that ghetto ass shit. So, I just started calling her Belle.

Belle had good hair and it made sense because my mom had hair past her shoulders. Lil Mama was cute. I could see I made pretty ass babies. I just hated who I made one with.

I pulled into a Walmart off 75 and decided to go ahead and get Belle some more diapers and baby wipes because I was out. I'd bought that shit four times since I had her and was running through it like notebook paper.

I circled the parking lot a few times hoping to find a spot closer to the front, so I didn't have to walk in this heat. Of course, this was the first of the month, so Walmart was packed and reminding me why I needed to invest in curbside delivery

After a few trips around the parking lot, I found a spot in the middle and backed into it the best I could while drunk. It took me a while because I wasn't in my right mind after a bottle of Hennessy.

Before I got out of the car, I reached into my glove compartment to spray some mint into my mouth. The shit was hot as hell and tasted way worse than the Hennessy, so I decided to take another shot.

"Whew, alright, let's go," I said to myself after wiping my hand across my lips and looking in the mirror. Just as I was getting out of the car, I got a call from an unknown number.

"Hello, who is this?"

"It's Treasure, Chris"

"Treasure? Where the fuck you at?"

"That's what I was calling you for. To let you know I'm okay. I'm over Cali's house. I accidentally fell asleep here last night. I also broke my phone, and it was already too late to get it replaced."

"Who the hell is Cali, Treasure?"

"Cali from the Miss Georgia pageant. She invited me here to work out with her yesterday and I lost track of time," she replied saying that as if there was nothing wrong.

"Treasure, you don't think you could've called me to let me know something. I mean, I have been out looking for you all night."

"I know Chris, I know. I just needed some time to myself. Don't I deserve to get a little peace after all this mess that's been going on?" she pleaded making me feel bad because this was all my fault. I felt for Treasure throughout this situation I really did, I was just hurt she didn't have compassion for me. She had no idea how much stress I was under. My life was crumbling right in front of my eyes.

"Look Treasure, I don't mind you having peace, but you can't run away from me forever. I love you; I want to marry you one day. I know we can work this out."

"Yeah well, all I ask is that you let me deal with this how I need to Chris. Maybe a couple of days away will make me see things in a new light. But please, don't try to rush my healing process. I do need time to heal," she said being the strong and stern Treasure I fell in love with.

"Okay baby whatever you say," I responded honestly relieved Treasure was still considering looking at shit from my perspective. That's all I wanted, and no one would ever have to know anything about Jalani Smith. Confessing truly was my last resort and something I didn't want to resort to.

"Well, I'll talk to you later. Cali and I are about to go have brunch."

"Okay Miss Georgia, I'll talk to you soon."

"Bye." She hung up the phone.

I was still drunk as fuck but hearing Treasure's voice made me feel ten times better. I felt like I had a boost of energy and could see the world a little clearer at this moment.

I grabbed my wallet, keys, and my phone then got out of the car into the scorching heat. Once the sun hit the back of my neck, I damn near jogged into the store sweating so badly. When I saw the subway sign, I knew that would be my first stop after I got everything I needed. I hadn't eaten all day but first I need to remember what I came here for.

Chapter 11

Deion

I was sitting on the front porch smoking my 4th blunt of the day. That's all I wanted to do today because I wasn't in the mood to have company the way I felt. I got my ass whooped last night by a nigga that was supposed to be my homie over a bitch he didn't even know. That shows you how funny niggas moved when it's pussy around.

There was no charging that shit to the game because he violated me in my own home, where my daughter and my baby mama live. I could only see out of one eye and the other one was as black as Wesley Snipes.

What Kaine doesn't realize is just because Treasure is Miss Georgia didn't make her off limits in the trap. I drug my baby mama on the regular when she getting on my nerves.

That nigga Kaine got a little money from a settlement, and now he thinks he's better than niggas in the hood. He was just like us though probably worse. That nigga had done some shit I would never do.

I only let the nigga think I respected him because I liked to use his studio for free from time to time.

I should burn that bitch down to the ground now that I'm thinking about it. Send a picture of the building up in flames on the side his granny mural is painted on. He didn't even like niggas leaning against that wall so I know setting it on fire would get to him.

Whatever I did for retaliation was well deserved, so I don't need anybody saying I'm wrong. Whether it be in his wallet or his body, Kaine was going to feel my pressure. As a matter of fact, when Coco's ass finally wakes up I had a story to tell her. This nigga was about to go from hero to villain quick and that shit he pulled last night would be for nothing.

Once I finished the blunt, I flicked it onto the grass, and then a car pulled up and Coco's client slash friend got out.

"Damn boy! What happened to your eye?"

"Damn girl, what happened to your baby daddy?" I asked making her smack her lips and proceed to knock on the door.

"What are you knocking for? It's open but she's in there sleep."

"Damn, she was supposed to do my hair at 2:00. I have to go to work at midnight," she said sitting down on the porch with a plastic bag filled with horsehair.

"For real Deion, what happened to your eye?"

"Why are you worried about me shawty? You got plenty niggas to worry about."

"Damn, okay sensitive much? I was just asking damn. No need to get smart." she replied as we both sat on the porch quiet for a second.

"Well, I got some cigars on me. Do you wanna smoke?" she asked tapping on that fake ass purse.

"Of course, you got cigars and probably no weed, the usual." I knew how this bitch rolled.

"Come on Deion don't play with me. I'll roll the blunt on your dick," she said, being her usual sneaky ass. Bitches like Shaniqua I didn't have to drug for pussy. All I had to do was simple shit like smoke a blunt with her and she was ready to fuck.

"How you gone roll a blunt on my dick shawty?"

"I'll break the cigar down and use it as my rolling tray," she put on a hoeish smirk.

I'd fucked this bitch more than a few times and she's aborted a couple of my babies. The first abortion I didn't think happened, but the second one was for real. I know because I went with her to make sure.

"Well, since you feel like that, then come on before Coco wakes up."

"That's what I like to hear but fuck the blunt. Let me just suck that shit first." She got excited. Every hoe in the hood was happy to fuck me because I'm a thug wrapped in tattoos. Before Kaine came around I was getting ninety-nine percent of the hoes around here. Now I was having to divide these thots by two.

"Come on, let's go around here," I said leading her to a secluded spot on the side of the house. There was an old pickup truck parked in front of the back gate which was full of junk fifteen feet high. With the car right there and us between the house and the shed, this was like a free motel room. This was all her pass-around ass was getting from me anyway. That and a mouth full of nut.

She went straight to unbuttoning my pants being all rough and shit.

"Damn shawty watch out, you moving a lil too fast, a nigga hurting," I said slowing her down as she grabbed my waist to pull down my shorts.

I noticed she stopped and looked at the bruise on my stomach. Grazing it with her finger and saying, "Damn."

I knocked her hand out of the way and put my dick in her mouth so she could shut the fuck up and do what we came back here to do. Once she got started, I was trying to appreciate her mouth but all I could think about was how this was supposed to be Treasure doing this shit to me last night, probably in the same place.

Shaniqua was sucking my dick so sloppy there was drool piling up on the chip bag directly underneath her mouth. I had to hold the wall to keep my balance.

"Damn, eat that dick baby. Just like that."

"You like that baby; I love sucking this dick" she replied licking it like an ice cream cone. All the pills in my system wouldn't let me nut right now but I was enjoying the hell out of shit.

"Coco, Deion is that y'all? Who back there, come help me with these groceries?" I heard my mother-in-law coming around the truck.

"Oh shit, get up," I said as me and Shaniqua attempted to look innocent, but we were already caught.

"Deion I just know you not back here with this hoe fucking around on Cocovani. Hell no! I'm about to go tell her so she can whoop this hoe ass!"

"Yo Juanita, Juanita, mother-in-law!" I said chasing her up to the front porch.

"Deion get away from me right now. You know you wrong for doing that outside y'all bedroom window."

"Listen, mother-in-law, just listen to me really quick. Please don't say anything to Cocovani. What do you need? Do you want to get your hair done? Some cigarettes, you want to go bingo?" I asked grabbing her by the arm. I heard the back gate rattling and saw Shaniqua damn near running away from the yard.

"I don't need anything from you! You can't think you can keep paying me off when my daughter is knocked out on pills and you fucking around on her. I thought you said you were going to help her get off that shit, but you ain't done nothing but make her addiction worse."

"Juanita, your daughter is stubborn and selfish, and you know that. I mean, why do you think I do shit like this? She is always knocked out on Xanax and can never show me attention. I just got jumped last night after the party because she owes a nigga some money for some pills, and I said I wasn't paying him."

"Lord Jesus." She shook her head and placed her hand on her hip.

"Juanita, I'm a nigga if I'm not anything else and when someone throwing it at me and your daughter never does, what am I supposed to do?"

"You need to do better, and she does too. The least you could do is take these hoes to the motels because I don't wanna see no shit like that again, do you hear me?"

"Yes ma'am. I hear you."

"Now make sure y'all clean that backyard up from the party. I'm having a card game back there next week."

"Yes ma'am, I will get right to it. Thank you." I walked away from her.

"Uh uh. Wait a minute, where you going?" she asked, sticking her hand.

"Where is my bingo money at?"

"Oh, I got you," I said, digging into my pocket.

"Thanks." She looked to the road before opening the screen door.

"Wait, isn't that my niece's car down the sidewalk? She still here?"

"No, I don't know why she left it there."

"Now she knows her mama going to have a fit if she knows she been in this area. She better hope she doesn't find out."

Juanita shrugged her shoulders and walked into the house. After she slammed the door, she immediately started bitching about the condition of the house and telling me to get the groceries out of the car.

I walked down the stairs too fast because I forgot I was hurt and sent immediate pain across my side. Every time I felt pain, I got mad all over again about last night.

Kaine isn't the only nigga who didn't tolerate disrespect and I was about to show him how disrespectful I can get. After getting the groceries, I went to the back of the house and grabbed two gas cans to fill up down the street. When the time comes, I want to be ready. His life is about to go up in flames

forever touching a nigga like me.

Chapter 12

Coco

In West Philadelphia born and raised

On the playground was where I spent

most of my days

"Ugh, Deion why is that TV so loud,
turn that shit down. And what smells like gas!"

"Man fuck that Coco, wake your ass
up. You sleep like you trying to die or
something," he said sitting next to me on the
bed. I laid my head back on the pillow and
attempted to drift back to sleep, but he started
shaking my leg, being more worrisome than his
daughter.

"Deion, I'm up!" I slurred fighting to open my eyes in this bright-ass room.

"Why did you open them curtains?"

"Cause you need to get your dumb ass up. I have been trying to wake you up for an hour."

"Okay, for what, and what time is it!" I said scrunching my face up at the stench of my own morning breath. I immediately noticed Deion's face was fucked up and he looked like Martin after Tommy the hitman Hearn beat his ass.

"Man, you need to check on your cousin."

"Check on her for what? And what happened to your face?"

"That nigga Kaine happened, that's what. Shawty I'm going to be real with you, your cousin a hoe," he said trying to give me way too much information and I'd just opened my eyes.

"Wait, what? You and Kaine got into a fight? Why did that happen and why is Treasure a hoe? Oh, fuck, did she do something wild because of that pill I gave her?" I asked with my hand over my mouth. I never planned on crashing myself, but obviously that one pill I took was way stronger than I thought. I know it must've had Treasure gone if it took me out because I wasn't a lightweight with Xanax. Lord, I hope I didn't put that girl in danger by being spiteful.

"I don't know if that was the only reason because I think you were right about her. She wild as hell and don't give a damn about family," he said sitting on the bed shaking his head. This nigga was being so dramatic, talking slowly, and I just wanted to know what happened.

"Deion, Talk! What happened last night?"

"Treasure started stripping in the living room and tried to fuck me."

"I knew that bitch would," I said getting the confirmation I already knew about my so-called cousin. She was checking for Deion the entire time and I knew it. She just needed a little medication to show it, and that's why I gave it to her.

"So why did you and Kaine fight?"

"Because he was trying to take that poor girl off all sloppy and shit. We battled it out, but I slipped and hit my head on the table. When I came to, they were gone," he said clinching the muscles in his jaw.

"Did she leave in her car?"

"No, it's still outside. Man, babe you might need to get in touch with her mom. After the way that nigga Kaine acted last night, I think he might actually be a rapist," Deion said talking about Kaine in a way I thought he never would.

I sighed deeply and pulled up Treasure's number to call her. I tried her phone six times in a row, and all my calls were left unanswered. I then tried Kaine's number from my phone and Deion jerked his neck back.

"How you know his shit?" He lifted an eyebrow as if he suspected something.

"You called me from his phone one night, remember?" I said trying to play it off. I was so anxious to see if Treasure was with Kaine I wasn't even thinking to ask Deion for Kaine's number but thank God he didn't make a big deal out of it.

I dialed Kaine's number back-to-back still getting no answer. He was probably deep in her guts this morning and that thought made my stomach hurt. Shit, I half-ass would've preferred she fucked Deion instead of Kaine. That's who I really wanted just for me.

Chapter 13

Chris

By the time I stumbled around Walmart and ate a ham, bacon, and cheese footlong, I was slumped in this booth. Who would've thought I would be here just a month ago? I had to climb out of this hole fast because I knew I looked bummy as hell right now. Halfway asleep hanging around a Walmart subway. I'm a doctor for God's sake.

When I heard a person barking over my shoulder I knew to lift my head.

"Yo, what's up my brother? Nigga in here tearing up a Subway sandwich I see," one of my old line brothers, Malik said, approaching the table with a redhead white girl. He was known in college to only prefer the bunnies and I was too before meeting Treasure her freshman year. I only snuck around with black chicks and made the white ones my girlfriend. Treasure was a good combination of both so that's why I made her mine.

"Katy, this the guy that's dating the girl who won Miss Georgia. Where is the beauty queen?"

"She's working out with a friend. Nice to meet you, Katy. What's going on with you though man? Long time no see." I replied, trying my hardest not to look as fucked up as I was. But this was my line brother. He knew when I was drunk.

"Nigga what are you doing in Walmart with diapers and shit, you and Treasure having a baby?" Malik questioned and it was like a light switch popped on in my head when he said diapers and baby. I then remembered I had Belle with me, and she had been in the car this whole time, I was tripping!

"Alright y'all, I gotta go!" I said grabbing the bag from the table and jetting out of the store.

"Yo! You dropped this bottle out!" Malik yelled attempting to stop me, but I was hustling to get to the car. It had to be 90 degrees at this point, and I'd been in Walmart for almost two hours. Belle was a newborn, and I knew better than anybody there were no conditions for her to be in. I was way past my limit today and all I could do was pray she was okay.

I ran as fast as I could to try and get to the car and turn the air on. When I made it there, the door was hot to the touch, and I was scrambling for my keys unable to get them out fast enough. Once I got the door unlocked, I pulled open my back passenger door and pulled back the covers that rested on top of Belle's skin.

"Come on Belle, I'm sorry lil one. I didn't mean to leave you in here," I said trying to discreetly check for a pulse. She was sweaty and unconscious and I couldn't find a pulse at all. My years of medical school let me know my worst nightmare; Belle was dead.

"No, no, come on Belle," I cried collapsing across onto her body. How could I have let this happen to an innocent baby? A child that was proven to be mine at that. I knew I couldn't show much emotion in the public parking lot, so I wiped tears away from my face and closed the car door.

My body felt numb, and I felt vomit building up in my throat at that very moment. I stood by the car throwing up everything inside me, which was mostly Hennessy and guilt. Now I was about to be facing jail time after something like this.

Chapter 14

Kaine

We sat on the couch watching reruns of Sanford and Son while the music played lightly in the background. This was some shit I could never stop watching because of my grandfather. He and I would watch this while Grandma was cooking breakfast on the weekends I spent with them in Atlanta. I missed the old times like a muthafucka. Especially that good-ass food my grandma used to make.

"Do you know how to cook?" I asked Treasure who was sitting with her back toward the arm of the couch with her feet facing me. Usually, I didn't like people's feet up on my furniture, but her toes were cute as shit. Simple and white just how I liked them.

"Sorta, but I know how to DoorDash even better," she said, doing that cute little giggle she had. When I asked her if was she ready to go to her car, she said no and got comfortable on my couch. She wasn't bothering me, and I wasn't messing with her. She seemed to be comfortable in my presence and hers was cool too. I hadn't chilled with a bitch like this since Jalani.

"Do you finally have the munchies after smoking that blunt? I was wondering when that would come?"

"Yeah, I'm hungry. I'm starving actually. That tea didn't do shit for me. I need some real food."

"That's so crazy that you drink tea, I never met a street dude that drinks tea."

"That's because you never met me and I'm not a street dude. I'm just a nigga from the streets," I said making her give me that little shy smirk she has been doing since yesterday.

Before she got drugged by that dumb ass nigga, she had been giving me that shy vibe all night. Somebody as pretty as her acting all innocent was rare. As beautiful as she is she should have all the confidence in the world. I'm nobody compared to her.

"So, what's your favorite kind of food?" She asked me.

"Anything that involves asparagus and a steak."

"You said that hella quick. Is that all you eat?"

"Yes that, and pussy," I said purposely messing with her to see that smirk again.

"You just had to be nasty, didn't you? Well, there's so many options other than steak and pussy Kaine. I say we eat at the 7th restaurant on DoorDash."

"Why the 7th?"

"Because it could be random and make both of us step outside of the box. I do it all the time. It helps me try new things. That's when I'm not dieting," she said while sliding her tongue across her juicy ass lips.

"Well let's do it then."

"Do what? It?" she questioned catching me off guard.

"Did you just say it?"

"I was kidding, but hand me your phone let's see what number seven is on there," she said reaching over to my phone that was on the armrest. When she stretched her body out across me, I got a peak of her ass cheeks that came from under my T-shirt I gave her. Plenty of hoes had slept in that shirt but nobody rocked it like Treasure.

When she sat back down, she sat on my hand by accident, but I didn't move.

"Here, unlock your phone, I'm not going to go through your messages or anything I promise."

"I don't care if you do. I'm not tied to anybody. You see what you see."

"Yeah, you say that now, but what about oh girl that just left?"

"I don't wanna talk about that bitch."

"Well, I understand that, because I don't want to talk about my situation back home either."

"What situation?"

"My boyfriend has a newborn baby that's not mine."

"Damn, your nigga stepped out on you? That tells me a lot."

"Excuse me? Tells you a lot about what?" she interrupted me becoming hostile.

"It tells me a lot about him shawty. He stepped out on you; he must be dumb. You seem chill, and you're not like all these other birds around Atlanta" I replied moving my hand from underneath her ass.

"Why thank you, Kaine. That means a lot." She kissed me on the cheek.

"But anyway, this situation opened my eyes about Chris. I thought he was the perfect guy but he wasn't. That negro didn't even use condoms with these girls. Now he is at home with a doorstep baby." She rolled her eyes, showing she had a little feistiness in her. I was still stuck on the kiss on the cheek, but I had to play it off. She kept talking as if it was platonic, so I knew not to get excited.

"Damn, that's what you call lil mama? A doorstep baby?" I laughed at her name for the kid.

"Yeah, but let me stop. I'm being ugly."

"Trust me, there ain't shit ugly about you. You really are gorgeous inside and out." I locked eyes with her, and she had a nigga stuck. Her smooth skin, pink lips, and perfect body was hard to ignore. But that face, she was so pretty I could look at her all day.

I bit my bottom lip and looked away because just that quick, I wanted to lick from the bottom of her toes to the top of her head.

It was crazy because I was starting to become thirsty for her. Something I swore I would never be in my life.

This was however Miss Georgia we talking about.

Chapter 15

Treasure

Two hours later

Wet, wasn't the word. More like sticky and slimy. Being this close to Kaine had me feeling a way and I wanted him so badly that I could taste him. I didn't care about the situation that got me here, I was just happy to be away from the real world. Over here I wasn't Miss' anything. I was just a girl chilling with a guy who happened to be the smoothest gangsta I'd ever met.

This boy was something special. He was like the thugs you read about in books that made you wet through the pages. His smooth rugged exterior was a perfect match for the calm soothing soul within. He didn't talk much, so I felt like I didn't have to either. We were just vibing with each other's energy and giving subtle seductive looks now and again. I see why Chris stepped out with some hood rat because I too was craving something new. Now I was wondering do hood rats fuck better than suburban girls and do gangstas fuck better than suburban guys.

"Hey Kaine, are ghetto girls better in bed than chicks not from the ghetto?"

He chuckled at my question.

"How would I know that? I haven't had both, yet. You should give me something to compare it to." he said making me bite my lip and clinch my pussy tightly.

"I bet I should." I batted my eyelashes at him,

I couldn't fuck Kaine today, it would be too soon. It hadn't even been twenty-four hours since we met, so I knew I would probably look like a hoe if we slept together. I mean, I am Miss Georgia. I couldn't be fucking random men on the first night.

I could never be in a real relationship with him anyway because he was a hood dude. I was supposed to be with a doctor or a lawyer, and not someone who would maybe need a lawyer one day. I just hated I had to think about my image while vibing with someone. I low-key couldn't wait to be free of this feeling.

We continued to sit comfy on his couch and ordered our food from DoorDash. The restaurant we chose was Buffalo Wild Wings and both had flavors we'd never eaten before. Kaine finally decided to turn off Sanford and Son and put it on my favorite movie Love and Basketball which was playing on BET. I didn't tell him; it was just like he knew. He was doing everything right and making me wanna sit right here forever.

I was eating slowly and watching the TV and Kaine out of the corner of my eye. I knew I was feeling him because even the way he ate his wings was sexy.

My mom had called his house phone back a few times, but I told her I would be here another night. She asked me about what happened between Chris and me and I told her a watered-down story about a fight we had. She tried telling me to go home and work it out, but I told her distance was what we needed. I hadn't heard from him since I called earlier anyway, so he was probably spending time with his baby mama.

I wasn't trying to overstay my welcome here, but he hadn't asked me to go yet, so I didn't plan on leaving. Kaine showed me with that girl earlier that when he wanted you to go you had to leave at that moment.

I finished up my meal and then used Kaine's iPad so I could log into my social media and check my email. Because of the rain Kaine said he was in for tonight and let me know I could stay here too if I wanted to.

Now we were chilling on his couch full of our meal and I really wanted to take a shower. I figured I might as well get comfortable since I was going to be here for another night.

"Do you have any clean towels?"

"Yeah shawty, why wouldn't I?"

"I don't know because maybe you could've used them all." I flirtatiously clapped back at him as he leaned back against the couch staring at me.

"They're in the closest located in the restroom, it's some bitch shit in there too."

"Bitch shit like what?"

"Soap, and razors and shit."

"Okay, thank you so much. I appreciate all the hospitality and you letting a stranger stay in your house."

"You're welcome, you are harmless. The only thing dangerous about you is your looks." He made me smile giving me that tingling feeling inside.

Maybe I may just surprise him when I get out of the shower and stop fighting the shit. I was horny and that chocolate man in there could get it.

I was being strong at first but honestly, I'm tired. I'm human and I want some dick.

Chapter 16

Coco

I'd called Treasure, and Kaine both like five times each, but I couldn't get an answer. My nerves were bad, and my hangover was severe all while trying to push through my client's head. I'd already missed her appointment earlier and now that she was back. I was sloppy and had to throw up every five minutes. I don't know how Dream's party turned into me getting drunk out of my mind, but I guess my cousin had my nerves that bad being a hoe and a sneak. Parts of me was hoping she was okay, but the envy in me didn't care. I didn't think Kaine would hurt her but according to Deion's bruised face, he went crazy last night.

After I came back from throwing up the last time, I took a long drink of water in hopes that I had taken my last trip to the bathroom.

"Bitch don't tell me Deion knocked you up again," Shaniqua asked.

"Girl, no. I'm nowhere near pregnant. I'm never letting Deion nut in me again."

"Girl, I hear that. My baby daddy thinks we going to keep fucking raw, but I told him I'm not on birth control and I'm not trying to have my 5th child," she said reminding me I was lucky to only have one.

"Speaking of baby daddies, where is yours?"

"He ran to the store and to the plug for some green. Why are you trying to make a purchase?" I asked knowing why she was checking for Deion. The pill heads were the only thing keeping us afloat with Deion spending our money for beats and shit. I wondered with him and Kaine fighting last night would he stop using his studio now.

"Nah, I'm good on that. Just asking. I haven't seen him in a while. But can I use the restroom? I had a daiquiri after I left your house earlier and it's running straight through me."

"Girl, go right ahead. You know where it is," I said finishing the last of a braid and letting Shaniqua get up from the chair. I sat down on the stool near the table and exhaled deeply wishing I was just in bed.

Shaniqua's phone was still playing music and that tired-ass Muni Long song Made For Me was playing for the 5th time. I grabbed her phone to hit skip and then a message preview popped up which grabbed my attention.

Yeah, I told you Coco don't know. Everythang cool. My mother-in-law not going to say shit either. I gave her money for bingo to keep hush.

I read from the message popping up on the screen. I immediately got skeptical because my mama had said she was going to Bingo tonight and didn't have any money just last night. I tried to hurry to the contact number when I heard the toilet flush in the nearby restroom. My heart raced worrying if my intuition was right this time. When I read the number, my heart stopped seeing it was my baby daddy's number attached to the message on Shaniqua's phone.

"These muthafuckas did not!?"

I said balling up my fist tightly trying to keep my composure as Shaniqua walked back into the room.

"Girl, you turned off that Made for me. That was my shit," she said walking her trifling ass back into the room.

I let her get comfortable in the chair and when she attempted to hand me some hair, I said,

"Let me see the whole pack on the floor."

She bent down to hand me the pack of hair and I popped the braiding hair from the cardboard packaging. After I got a good grip on both ends, I turned it into a weapon and wrapped it around Shaniqua's dusty ass neck trying to kill this bitch!

"Hoe I saw that message from Deion! You fucking my baby daddy bitch!" I said holding the hair around her neck so tightly it was stretching in my hand but still choking the shit out of her. She was struggling and squirming trying to get her airways open, but I wasn't playing with this hoe. I will kill this bitch.

"Do you know I will kill you bitch!" I screamed holding on tighter and tighter as she clawed into my hands breaking them cheap ass nails. Just as she was about to lose consciousness, I let her go and then started beating the hell out of her.

"Hey! Hey! What the fuck going on in here!" Deion yelled coming through the front door. He most likely heard the commotion from outside and didn't know he was the cause of it.

"Yo Coco, what the fuck you doing?"

"Shut up trifling ass nigga! You next!" I said charging toward him and giving him that same aggression.

"Coco what are you talking about!"

"Deion shut the fuck up! I saw the messages you just sent her while in my chair dumb ass! How could you mess around with my friend!"

"Baby I'm sorry, look let's just get this bitch out of here and talk about this shit in private," he said grabbing my arms.

"There is nothing left to talk about! You and that bitch can go and my mama's ass too!"

"Man, Coco you can't turn on your family! We have been living here as a family all these years!"

"And I don't care! I've been taking care of y'all all these years! When we lost the last apartment, I was the one who got the housing voucher! This is my shit! Y'all not even supposed to be here!" I screamed more pissed than I had ever been before.

"Bitch quit squirming and get off the floor before I wax your ass again," I said kicking Shaniqua in her stomach. Deion's dumb ass was still standing in my house, so I got a knife to remove him.

"Nigga how many times I have to say get the fuck out!"

"Okay, Coco. Damn, I'm leaving!" he said putting his hands up when I pulled out that butcher knife. I was on a war path right now and the jealousy festering in me was turning into rage. Everybody seemed to be on some snake shit. It was time I start moving like one.

After I helped put all of his shit in a box to
the left, I dismissed him and text my mama
to come get her shit too. It was already bad she
wasn't half of a mother to me and an even worse
grandma to Dream. Now she's getting bribes
from my man to keep secrets from me. There's
honestly no telling what I would be if
I wasn't her child. Probably on the stage with
Treasure instead of envying her from the
crowd.

I was in my feelings deeply and just wanted my mind to be on something better, someone better. I wanted that person who could help cleanse my mind, body, and soul. I don't give a fuck what my hoe-ass cousin did with him last night, I needed to see Kaine like now. I wasn't going to just let her take him because I had him first. Side nigga or not, that was my dick and I needed it now.

I decided to call Kaine once again to see if he would answer. I was shocked when the phone finally picked up after calling him all day.

"What's up?" he answered the phone making me nervous as hell from hearing his strong commanding tone.

"Hey Kaine, it's Coco... uhh, is my cousin over there?" I asked probably sounding as nervous as I was.

"No, I took her home this morning. Why? What's going on?"

"Nothing, I was just wondering if you were alone," I replied, and the phone line went quiet for a moment.

"Ayee, I have to take this other call. I will hit you back later, aiight."

"Okay," I responded and Kaine immediately hung up the phone.

He sounded as if he were home, and I would probably have a better shot of sleeping with him if I just showed up at his place with no panties on.

Tonight was about to be about me, and my body and I wanted to release all my frustrations on Kaine. I know Treasure couldn't fuck better than me.

Chapter 17

Treasure

This bath and him waiting in the other room made me feel so sexy. I felt so smooth and so refreshed after using whatever bitches exfoliating body scrub on my legs and thighs.

I grabbed a towel from the top rack in the linen closet and wrapped it around my body. I was about to walk out in front of Kaine just to see his reaction to my long hair against my naked shoulders.

I both felt and smelled like a million bucks and decided in the shower I would have sex with Kaine tonight. Yes, he was a stranger to me, but he was the type of gentle I needed in my life.

I brushed through my hair a few more times and placed the brush on the counter. I was about to walk out of the restroom when I looked into the mirror and saw Jalani's name embroidered on the towel I was wearing.

I quickly removed the towel from my body and sat it back on the top shelf. I grabbed another towel and checked it for names before wrapping it around my body. I looked in the mirror one last time and then walked out the door.

Kaine was standing in the kitchen and stopped mid-sip from his cup of water to lick his lips.

"You need a shirt? You can look in the top drawer by the nightstand to get another one," he said trying not to stare too hard.

I shook my head and responded, "I'm fine." Then I made my way to the couch to have a seat. Once I got to the couch, I realized I was thirsty both figuratively and literally.

"Where are your cups? I need something to quench my thirst?"

"In the cabinet to the left of the stove."

"Okay cool." I walked into the kitchen. The sexual tension between us was so high right now I didn't feel like fighting it anymore.

"Kaine?"

"Yeah?"

"Can you hold this?" I asked, giving him the towel from around my body. The way his eyes lit up; I knew he appreciated my naked frame in front of him. He looked at me like he was studying every inch of my body and making mental notes of where he wanted to kiss.

"Treasure, if you not trying to feel every inch of me, you might want to put your towel back on," he said shaking his head slowly.

"Well, do you think I would be naked in your kitchen right now if I didn't want to feel every inch of you?" I said walking up and Kaine wrapped his beautiful chocolate frame around my body.

"Damn. Now this is more like it." I said rubbing my hands down to his already hard dick.

"Man, shawty why have you been playing with me all day? If you wanted me to give you dick you should've just said that."

"Well, I'm saying it now Kaine," I said wrapping my arms around his neck.

"So, you giving me permission now to tear your ass up?" he asked being his same cocky self.

"Yes, I am."

"Good, because that's exactly what I have been wanting to hear," he said kissing me on my lips. We started intertwining our tongues into one another kissing like teenagers that were in love. His lips were just as fresh and minty as I imagined, soft yet firm and sending waves down to my pussy. He was just as aggressive as I knew he would be, picking me up from the floor and carrying me to the bedroom. He started kissing me in places I'd never been kissed before and making me feel like this was my first time, even though it was just my first time with him.

Kaine kissed down my body and started eating my pussy and I knew right then he was nothing to play with. Where I thought Chris ate pussy good, he never did it like this and I felt like I couldn't control myself. Kaine was using his tongue, his lips, and his fingers to please me and I was squirming like a snake. After only a minute I was running up the headboard as I came on his tongue.

He pulled me back down to his face saying, "Where the fuck are you going?" While putting me right back in my place.

Kaine didn't stop eating me until he wanted to. I came twice on his face, but he never stopped going. When he finally got up, he removed his shirt from his built-ass body letting his dick free of his shorts.

Before now, I'd only suck one man's dick, so this was new for me, this size especially. I took his dick into my mouth and closed my eyes going to work because I knew I had to. Kaine deserved the best head ever after what he gave me.

He didn't have hair on his balls, so I made sure to take them into my mouth just to prove my point. I knew I wasn't a rookie, but I'd only been with Chris before, so I hoped I was good at what I did. I mean, Chris did step out on me so my head game couldn't have been all that. I don't know though, Kaine seemed to be enjoying it. He was very vocal about it too.

"Fuck, Treasure. Shit," he said moaning my name and saying subtle cuss words as I swallowed his dick. I know he wasn't faking it because there wasn't shit fake about Kaine. When he moved my head and bust the biggest load ever, I knew I had done my job.

"Climb on this dick."

He said, and I did just as he asked. Sliding down his dick I bit on my bottom lip unable to fathom how much dick was inside me at the moment.

"Take this dick. This what you wanted, huh?" he said, sitting back against his headboard as I bounced on him. I was holding on to this nigga for dear life because he was in my guts right now. This man already had me hooked and we were only two minutes in.

After riding him for at least thirty minutes I got on my knees, and he started hitting me from the back. He was so gentle and so aware of what I wanted talking me through the initial pain.

"Arch your back a little more. Yeah, that's it." He slid deeper inside my walls. I was thick with Kaine, and he felt so good inside me. He started off slow and as he got deeper, he stroked faster. After a few minutes, I started to shake having my first vaginal orgasm ever. I realized now that I've come, but never had an orgasm before. I shook immensely like a vibrator and when my body calmed down, I could feel Kaine kissing down my back.

When I stopped shaking, I was turned on my back and Kaine climbed in between my legs to fuck me from the front. He looked me into my eyes as he slid inside my walls until our stomachs touched.

"Let me know if I go too deep alright."

"Okay, but I don't think you will," I replied before he kissed my lips. This was in fact how soul ties formed because I was already feeling them right now. After all, his dick was long enough to travel up to my soul with just one stroke.

Chapter 18

Coco

After taking a shower, giving myself a fresh shave, and straightening my hair I was on my way to Kaine's house. I only knew where he stayed because I'd picked Deion up from there one night after they'd gone to Magic City. The address was still saved in my search history, and I'd taken a screenshot just in case I needed it.

When Kaine said he was home alone I couldn't control the urge to get over to his house. I know it probably made me no better than Deion but so be it. I was a woman scorned.

When I parked outside his house, I walked up to the door and took a deep breath before I knocked, After I knocked a few more times I heard a door shut on the inside and the locks started to turn.

"Coco, what's up? What you doing here?" he asked after swinging the door open.

"Umm, I came to talk to you, feel you, swallow your cum." I said rubbing up the front of his chest. Kaine didn't have a shirt on and was sweaty as hell like he'd been working out.

"So, can I come in?"

"Nah, I don't think it's a good time right now."

"Why? I thought you were alone. Or did someone beat me over here?"

"To be honest, Treasure is still here and we kinda busy right now," Kaine said placing those cold ass words in my ears not knowing how fragile that made me.

"So that's how it is? You're dissing me for my cousin?" I snapped quickly expressing my jealousy.

"Coco, don't you got a nigga? You can't be sweating me shawty. Treasure cool and I'm dealing with her right now."

"Oh, so you think you're going to be with Treasure. Ha! That's laughable! Kaine no matter how innocent you may have been, Treasure and her mom will still look at you like a convicted rapist and never show your face to the world like that other girl didn't. Be her secret if that's what you want."

"Man watch out," he said attempting to shut the door in my face. By this time, I was pissed and reckless.

"What, do you think she's going to claim you in public? Do you think my aunt will let her!" I started getting louder and louder.

"Man, Coco get away from my door with that bull shit. I'm not your nigga so you need to go find him and give him this same energy. He tried to fuck her last night too. The only difference is she wanted me to have it and he was trying to take it." he said closing the door and locking both the locks.

My face was stuck on stupid, and I stood there for a minute green with envy. Somehow this was all coming back to Treasure and how I never should've had her at my house. Now I felt alone and isolated with no one to run to. Not my man, not my friend, and not my mom which hurt the most. Standing outside Kaine's door right now I felt lower than low, hurt and used. I knew there was nothing left to do but bring Treasure down from that high horse she'd been on all her life. Her ass caused this, and the world was about to see what kind of woman she really was.

I walked away from the door and pulled out my phone to find Chris's name on Facebook. If I had to deal with knowing Treasure was fucking Kaine, so did he. She wasn't about to make my side nigga her side nigga and her man doesn't know. I was done giving a fuck about her.

It was time to start exposing that bitch for real.

When I got back home, I swooped into the driveway and got out of my car just in time to catch my mama coming out of the house.

"Coco, guess who I saw coming from behind your grandfather's old truck."

"Save it, Juanita, I already know what you did and it's foul because you are supposed to be my mother. I want you out by tomorrow. I know you saw my text message."

"Really Coco?"

"Yes, really!"

I snapped, letting her know exactly how I felt. Me and my mama's relationship never had much strain saying she always let me do what I wanted. Now, in a way, I blamed her for the way I turned out. I for sure wasn't letting Dream do what she wanted her whole life because children need structure. Me and Corey were good examples of that. At least he wasn't lost in the system just yet.

"So, you're going to put me out and not that nigga?"

"He has to get the fuck out too. But I'm disgusted with you the most mama. You are supposed to love me unconditionally and have my back like no other, not him. Corey can stay here, but you have to go. Get your shit and get the fuck out." I left her on the front porch looking stupid. I was done with her ass along with a lot of other mutha fuckas in my life.

Chapter 19

Chris

I'd drove as far as I could listening to the radio play the same songs in rotation. My mind was in another space which made my thoughts hazy and I was in highway hypnosis.

Belle's dead body still laid in her car seat in the back, and I hated the thought of what I was going to have to do with her. She was an innocent baby who deserved a proper burial as would any other little angel on earth. I was a doctor, I was supposed to save people, not be the reason they die.

When I first found Belle's dead body, I knew my fault in it all was enough to be charged with murder. I got drunk and left a newborn baby in the car for hours in the middle of a hot Georgia day.

Megan was somewhere thinking she had one upped me by dropping our baby off, now her child was dead, and she didn't even know it. She would never know what happened to Belle because I was going to tell her I never found her and came home to nothing there. She blocked me on everything possible, so she had no proof I was trying to contact her, and I was going to delete all the footage from the Ring account and throw that mutha fucka in the trash. In the end, she would look like the terrible parent that left her daughter outside and she got abducted.

I was now driving to find the perfect spot to bury her body. No matter where I put her, she wouldn't be in a casket but a plastic bag which made me feel even more like a monster. After driving for a good minute, I felt I found the perfect spot down by some trees and a creek. I'd picked up a shovel at an old country store with no cameras and even got a rose from a lady on the side of the road to put on her grave. When I pulled the car over, I broke down crying before I pulled myself together. This was hard as hell for me.

I got out of the car and walked down the hill with the light from my phone. Holding it under my chin I tapped the ground twice to see if the dirt was loose enough for me to dig. I took one deep plunge into the ground and was already feeling sweat falling down my face. I was about to go for another dig when I damn near pissed on myself seeing red and blue lights shine on the creek.

I immediately chucked the shovel in the water and unzipped my pants pulling my dick out to act as if I was peeing.

"Hey, hands up down there!" I heard a cop say as he held a flashlight in his hand.

"Yes, sir officer sir. I'm wrapping it up in just one moment. Too much lemonade on the road," I said as piss actually started to flow.

"Hurry up and put your hands up!" he yelled shining the flashlight toward me along with his gun.

This was Georgia, and I was a black man out at night. I would still be scared shitless even if there wasn't a dead baby in the car and a shovel two yards away from me in the creek.

I raised my hands to the sky and stood there with my penis out praying that I didn't get shot or arrested.

"Sorry officer, I'm just out here taking a leak. Going to visit some family in Savannah," I said speaking as professionally as I could.

"Come up toward me boy and keep your hands in the air," he cut the small talk short with me.

"Yes sir," I responded feeling an immediate lump form in my throat.

He patted me down and asked if I had any weapons as we stood there in the headlights.

"Alright, put your private parts up now." I did as he asked.

"Do you know how dangerous it is being parked on the side of the road this late at night, especially in this location? This is a blind spot, and no one can see you parked here as they're going sixty miles per hour around that corner. Now, it looks like you got a car seat in the back with you. You're putting you and your baby at risk," he said flashing the light toward the backseat where Belle was.

"Yes sir, I understand that now. I'm sorry I wasn't thinking sir. I was just trying not to have my baby smelling my piss the entire trip if I peed myself," I said trying to laugh it off hearing my conscience eating me alive.

"Well, don't do anything like this the rest of the trip. Now go ahead and get back on the road. There's a gas station every 20 miles on this highway. Use the restroom there boy," he said walking back toward his car as I got into mine. I sat back in my seat and exhaled deeply before the officer flashed his lights for me to pull off.

I did so and the stress began to pile up once again. My day seemed to be getting harder and harder when I thought it was getting better after first hearing from Treasure.

Now I was back at square one and feeling just as defeated as when Megan left Belle at my doorstep. I couldn't do anything but cry real tears because the pressure I was feeling was worse than anything before.

I probably needed to get a motel and rest for tonight. Belle would just have to go inside the trunk until I figured out another place to take her.

Ping. Ping. I heard coming from my phone. It was the Facebook app with a notification that I had a message from Coco, Treasure's cousin. What the fuck could she want? When I passed by a gas station. I pulled over to check her message in case she was sending word for Treasure.

Hey, can you call me? I have to tell you about your girlfriend and where she's been. You're a good dude and she doesn't deserve you.

I read it over and over again. Was this shit for real?

Chapter 20

Treasure

The next morning

I don't think I ever had sex so good that I thought about it all night when I should've been asleep. My arm was wrapped around Kaine's body, and his light snore was just as peaceful as the sound of the fan in my room. This was my second morning waking up here and it felt comfortable. It felt right.

When the house phone started ringing, I knew it was for me. Kaine let me know no one called him so I knew it had to be my mother up bright and early trying to keep tabs on me. I got out of bed and walked over to the phone rolling my eyes as I picked it up.

"Yes Mom," I said whispering as Kaine flipped over disturbed by her calls.

"Treasure, it's your mom. They just called me from the hospital about Grandpa Thomas. Things took a turn for the worse last night and now Grandpa is on a breathing machine. They wanna know if we wanna pull the plug on him because he had another stroke and he is brain-dead. I gotta do it Treasure, I can't let him lay there and suffer like that," my mom said breaking down on the phone. I shut my eyes and started to cry too.

"Oh my god mama, I'm so sorry. Where are you now? Are you okay?" I

asked concerned about my mother's well-being. She's been taking care of Granddaddy since before I can remember. Besides me, he was her whole life. She had been the best daughter in the world to him and despite what my family thought, she was doing it from a kind place in her heart. Not for his money.

"I'm alright baby. I'm on my way to the hospital now. You need to get here sweetie. I've called the rest of the family as well. We all gotta say goodbye," my mom cried as I held the phone crying as well.

"You good Treasure?" Kaine asked and I immediately covered the speaker with my hand.

"Yeah, it's just my grandpa is brain-dead,"
I replied and he dropped his head. I could see he
didn't know what to say.

"Mom I'll be on my way up there in a
minute. I need to get taken to my car."

"Where is your car, Treasure?"

"It's at the gym, we didn't want to drive
two cars to Cali's,"

"Well sweetie, don't worry about your car,
just come straight here. I want you to be able to
see him before they unplug the machine.
He's being cremated you know." she
said making me drop even more tears thinking
about my grandpa.

"Okay mama, I'll be there," I replied and
hung up the phone with a heavy heart.

I loved my granddad and my grandma so much growing up and I'd already lost her to cancer years ago. Everything was supposed to be perfect in my life right now, yet things were constantly going wrong. It seemed like ever since I won that pageant bad stuff has been happening to me. It was like I was cursed or maybe it was just karma for how I got the title in the first place.

"You okay? Where do you need me to take you?" Kaine got down on one knee in front of me.

"The hospital. They are about to pull the plug on my grandpa, and I need to see him before they take him away. Can you take me up there?" I said crying uncontrollably at this point.

"Of course I can. Let me get dressed." He got up from the floor and I quickly put on my clothes. I was happy that I wasn't alone because my hands were shaking, and I couldn't drive right now anyway. Kaine had no idea how much I appreciated him right now. Everything he's done for me the past couple of days won't go unnoticed.

We made it to the hospital in no time with Kaine's fast driving and I was happy for it. He pulled me into the parking lot just in time to catch more of my family getting out of their cars.

"Thank you for bringing me up here."

"No problem beautiful."

"Here, write your number down on this napkin and I'll call you later."

I have him a pen and a napkin.

"Alright, and I'm sorry again about your grandpa. Death is such a fucked-up unexpected thing," he said looking at me with those beautiful comforting eyes.

"Thanks, Kaine, I'll see you soon for sure," I grabbed his cheek as I thanked him. Though circumstances tried to get in the way of us enjoying each other, we still bonded all day and made love all night. Being around Kaine was what I needed, and he'd been the perfect gentleman from the jump. I knew I couldn't scream to the world that he was mine but so far, I wanted him in my life.

I kissed Kaine on his lips and got out of the car just in time to catch Coco who was walking up with Dream on her hip.

"Hey Coco. I can't believe this is happening with Grandpa. He went downhill so fast," I said damn near jogging to catch up with Coco. She'd seen me coming toward her and turned her head walking away from me like she didn't know who I was.

"Coco, wait up!"

"What Treasure! Leave me the fuck alone, I don't have anything to say to you."

"Why?" I stood appalled by her attitude.

"You heard what I said, get away from me. I'm here for my grandpa and grandpa only. I don't have to talk to you or bow down to your ass so move," she snapped storming off before I could say a word.

"Coco stop, talk to me. What did I do," I asked grabbing her arm from behind.

"I don't know what happened the other night, but I apologize for any actions that may have offended you. I heard I was drugged."

"Girl bye. You know you need to check yourself and stop fronting like you're someone you're not!"

"And what does does that mean?"

"It means you're Miss Georgia but that still doesn't take away from the fact that you're a slut who can't control herself after one drink."

"It wasn't just drinks, apparently someone gave me Xanax."

"One drink, or pills, it really doesn't matter. You're miss perfect with that crown on your head but when it's off you're just like everybody else. Same problems and the same fucked up ways. You couldn't help but try to hoe your way around the hood and try to sleep with Deion and Kaine last night," she said catching me completely off guard.

"Excuse me?"

"And who told you about being drugged, Kaine?"

"Yeah, he did but."

"But nothing, use your college brain Treasure. Kaine gave you those pills, got you to his house, and fucked you while you were still unconscious. Then let me guess. You woke up this morning and fucked him again this time sober. Your mama would be disappointed in you."

She tore into me like she hated my guts. I wanted to cry and punch her in the face at the same time because she destroyed my feelings. Not only that, but this girl was lying and putting the blame on me and Kaine when her baby daddy was the reason for all of this.

"Coco if you're insinuating Kaine did that to me then you're wrong. He wouldn't do any shit like that. But Deion, oh we know he would."

"And how the fuck do you know that, Treasure? You don't know either one of them."

"But I've been around both and spent even more time with Kaine the past couple of days. What you are saying happened isn't in his character."

"You don't know his fucking character, please."

"I know he saved me when you were too fucked up to look out for me. That's if you even cared. You probably wanted to see me violated so I could be pathetic just like you!" I yelled, way past my boiling point.

Suddenly, I heard commotion in the back which got my attention.

"You know what you did Lisa! You wanted him dead so you could collect that money! You needed it to fund that prom queen! You know you poisoned my daddy!"

I heard Aunt Juanita's voice.

We ran up to the commotion where my aunt and my mom were

exchanging words being held away from one another. It was like Grandpa's dying was affecting everyone at this moment. Even our moms are going at it.

"Mama, what's going on?"

"That bitch is stupid Treasure, that's what's going on. She's saying I was poisoning your grandfather when I've done nothing but take care of him since the day Mama passed ten years ago!"

"Girl, please! I knew my daddy was going to be dead within six months after you took out that life insurance policy! You're not fooling me, Lisa!" Aunt Juanita yelled about a policy I knew nothing about.

"Look, Juanita, if you ever came to check on your father you would see that he's been withering away for a long time. But no, you couldn't do that. You were too busy scrapping up money to gamble or to give to that sorry nigga you laid up with!"

"Okay," Coco added as if she were agreeing with my mom.

"Anyways, as I said in there over my father's body, I will be contacting the detective as soon as I get home to look into his death. You're not about to collect money again at the expense of one of my parents dying. I just won't have it. You truly lost your soul trying to make this girl Miss fuckin America" My aunt pointed in my direction.

"Whatever Juanita, do what you gotta do, but you're wrong as hell for wanting them to cut Daddy's body open for no reason!"

"Because you want to burn his body for no reason! Or wait, there is one. You want him to get cremated to get rid of evidence. Since when did Daddy want to be cremated?" My Aunt Juanita replied, and my mother started shaking her head.

"Jealousy, that's all this is about is jealousy. You've been jealous of me since we were kids Juanita!"

My aunt stood there staring a hole through my mama as if she wanted to kill her.

"You know what Lisa, kiss my ass and go to hell because you are nothing to be jealous of! You've always thought you were better than me because of your good grades. From the moment I turned 18 and had the twins, you looked down on me! You threw it in my face that I needed help with them!" my Aunt Juanita said getting super emotional as she spoke to my mom.

"Wait, what twins mama? I was born when you were 18 years old." Coco chimed in.

"Coco and Treasure, it's time we tell you this."

"Don't do this Juanita. Today is not the day, I beg you." My mama said pleading with my aunt.

"Treasure your mama should've been told you this and she promised me she would one day. Instead, she lied to you all these years and made everybody else around you lie to keep a secret," she said making me nervous the more she spoke.

"What are you talking about Aunt Juanita?"

"Lisa, are you going to tell her?"

"You're a low-down dirty dog. These girls have nothing to do with this."

"Yes, they do. It's time they know the truth."

"Look everything I've done for Treasure was out of love for her! I've always wanted to protect her from anything that could hurt her. I'm her protector!" my mom said crying as she spoke to Aunt Juanita.

"Protect her, girl, please! You've been putting that child through hell since she was two, dressing her up like a doll taking away her entire childhood! You kept her away from family for years after you promised you would never do that. You made her whole life about them damn pageants and didn't give a damn if she was even breathing or not. She really did need protecting but it was from you, I should've been the one who protected her!"

"How do you feel you could protect her from me? You have some fucking nerve, Juanita!"

"Because I'm her mother, that's why!" Juanita yelled toward my mom who immediately looked toward me.

"Mama, what the fuck are you talking about?" Coco asked the question I couldn't even get out of my mouth.

"Treasure is your sister Coco, your twin sister," she said dropping a bomb as the rest of the hospital seemed to go silent.

"I gave her to your Aunt Lisa because she found out she couldn't have any kids at an early age, and I was overwhelmed. I gave this woman the beauty of being a mother and she still treated me like shit! She wouldn't even let you two take pictures together because she was afraid people would see just how much you two looked alike! She made up the story about being raped just so Treasure wouldn't ask about her daddy!" Juanita spat as I began to back away from the group. Coco started to shake her head and turned to leave at the exact moment as I did.

"Treasure, baby wait! Wait let me explain!" my mom shouted as I ran out the

door and toward the parking lot. I ran so long my mama couldn't keep up with me and I was able to escape her excuses.

When I got to the nearby McDonald's, I asked to use the phone so that I could call Kaine. I needed an escape more now than ever. I never wanted to see any of them ever again. My entire life has been a lie.

Chapter 21

Kaine

We rode away from the McDonald's pretty much in silence as Treasure cried silently in the passenger seat. I was confused as to what happened in just five minutes of her being there.

We pulled into my driveway, and I had no intention of staying when we got there. If Treasure wanted to chill out here that was fine by me. Spending time with her, reminded me of times with Jalani. I hated to compare the two, but it was the truth.

When I pulled into my parking spot, Treasure took off her seatbelt,

"I'm about to run around and do some shit for a minute. You can go in the crib, and I'll be back later." I said attempting to grab my house key from the keychain.

"Okay Kaine, but there's something I need to ask you."

"Yeah, what's up?"

"I'm not trying to get in your business but why did you spend time in prison?"

"Where I don't wanna talk about this shit for the millionth time in my life, I guess I have to. I was caught up with somebody that wasn't good for me. When I wasn't fucking with Shawty no more she said I raped her, and her daddy get me convicted. They got DNA evidence planted to make it look like I raped five women, and I was locked up for four years. I was rotting in that muthafucka until her roommate at Georgia State, who was Jalani, turned her in when she admitted to everything one night."

"So, she lied to you, and they found out it was a lie?"

"Yeah."

"And Jalani, as in Jalani Smith? Is that how you two met?"

"Yeah, and that's why I cut for her so hard. She was legit a nigga's saving grace."

Just thinking about that shit instantly got me in a terrible mood. It was like I could never leave it in my past because people kept bringing it up. I never wanted to think about that or Lani because it hurt too bad. I was tough, but that shit affected me every day.

"I'm about to roll out. Are you going in or back to your car? It's not safe for you to ride around with me."

"I don't even care about that car right now. I'll go inside."

"Okay, I'll be back later. Here, let yourself in.

I responded as Treasure reached for the door. She second-guessed herself and then doubled back to kiss me on the lips grabbing my face as we kissed.

BOOM. BOOM. BOOM.

Somebody started beating at the car window.

"Treasure get out of the car now! This what you doing," a man yelled beating on my car window like he was dumb.

"Chris!" Treasure said looking out of the window. She opened the door and got out of the car, and I did too. Who the fuck is this nigga?

"Chris, did you follow me here?"

"I was given the address! I should've known you were fucking around on me too. You gave me all this grief about what I did and you with this thug ass nigga." He pointed at me.

"Nigga you got five seconds to get the fuck away from my house or I'm going to hurt you." I got face to face with him because I don't know who this nigga thought he was. However, at that moment I realized that I recognized him from somewhere. He was the same nigga that followed me and Jalani around the grocery store the last time I saw her. I would never forget this nigga face.

I put the gun up to his head making Treasure start to scream.

"You did something to Jalani didn't you? Didn't you!"

To be continued

A Beauty Queen's Millionaire

Gangster 2

Made in the USA
Coppell, TX
19 November 2024